THE GIRL WHO PLAYED GO

Shan Sa was born in 1972 in Beijing. She left China for
France in 1990, studied in Paris and worked for two
years for the painter Balthus. Her two previous novels
were awarded the Prix Goncourt du Premier Roman and
the Prix Cazes.

Shan Sa

THE GIRL WHO PLAYED GO

TRANSLATED BY
Adriana Hunter

V

VINTAGE

Published by Vintage 2004

2 4 6 8 10 9 7 5 3 1

First published in French in 2001 as
La Joueuse de go by
Editions Bernard Grasset, Paris, France

First published in Great Britain in 2003 by
Chatto & Windus

Vintage
Random House, 20 Vauxhall Bridge Road,
London SW1V 2SA

Random House Australia (Pty) Limited
20 Alfred Street, Milsons Point, Sydney
New South Wales 2061, Australia

Random House New Zealand Limited
18 Poland Road, Glenfield,
Auckland 10, New Zealand

Random House (Pty) Limited
Endulini, 5A Jubilee Road, Parktown 2193,
South Africa

The Random House Group Limited Reg. No. 954009
www.randomhouse.co.uk/vintage

A CIP catalogue record for this book
is available from the British Library

ISBN 0 09 944498 4

Papers used by Random House are natural, recyclable
products made from wood grown in sustainable forests.
The manufacturing processes conform to the environ-
mental regulations of the country of origin

Printed and bound in Great Britain by
Bookmarque Ltd, Croydon, Surrey

1

I N THE Square of a Thousand Winds the frost-covered players look like snowmen. White vapour billows from their mouths and noses, and icicles growing along the underside of their fur hats point sharply downwards. The sky is pearly and the crimson sun is sinking, dying. Where does the sun go to die?

When did this square become a meeting place for go players? I don't know. After so many thousands of games, the chequerboards engraved on the granite tables have turned into faces, thoughts, prayers.

Clutching a bronze hand-warmer in my muff, I stamp my feet to thaw out my blood. My opponent is a foreigner who came here straight from the station. As the battle intensifies, a gentle warmth washes through me. Daylight is dwindling and the stones are almost indistinguishable. Suddenly someone lights a match and a candle appears in my opponent's left hand. The other players have all left and I know that Mother will be sick with worry to see her daughter come home so late. The night has crept down from the sky and the wind has stirred. To protect the flame, the man shields it with his gloved hand. From my pocket I take a flask of clear spirit which burns my throat. When I put it under the stranger's nose, he looks at it incredulously. He is bearded and it's hard to tell his age; a long scar runs from the top of his eyebrow and down through his right eye, which he keeps closed. He empties the flask with a grimace.

There is no moon tonight, and the wind wails like a new-born baby. Up above us, a god confronts a goddess, scattering the stars.

The man counts the stones once and then twice. He has been beaten by eighteen points; he heaves a sigh and hands me his candle. Then he stands up, unfolding a giant's stature, picks up his luggage and leaves without a backward glance.

I stow the stones in their wooden pots. They are crisp with frost in my fingers. I am alone with my soldiers, my pride gratified. Today, I celebrate my one hundredth victory.

2

MY MOTHER, being small, only comes up to my chest, and prolonged mourning for her husband has dried her out. When I tell her I have been posted to Manchuria, she pales.

'Mother, please, it is time your son fulfilled his destiny as a soldier.'

She withdraws to her room without a word.

All evening her devastated shadow is silhouetted against the white paper screen. She is praying.

This morning the first snows fell on Tokyo. Kneeling with my hands flat on the tatami, I prostrate myself before the altar of my ancestors. As I come back up I catch sight of the portrait of venerable Father: he is smiling at me. The room is filled with his presence – if only I could take a part of it all the way to China!

My family is waiting for me in the living room, sitting on their heels and observing a ceremonial silence. First of all, I say goodbye to my mother, as I used to as a child when I left for school. I kneel before her and say,

'Okasama,[1] I am leaving.' She bows deeply in return.

I pull on the sliding door and step out into the garden. Without a word, Mother, Little Brother and Little Sister follow me out. I turn round and bow down to the ground. Mother is crying and I hear the dark fabric of her kimono rustling as she bows in turn. I start to run. Losing her composure, she launches herself after me in the snow.

I stop. So does she. Afraid that I might throw myself into her arms, she takes one step back.

'Manchuria is a sister country,' she cries. 'But there are terrorists trying to sour the good relations between our two emperors. It is your duty to guard this uneasy peace. If you have to choose between death and cowardice, don't hesitate: choose death!'

We embark amid tumultuous fanfares. Soldiers' families jostle with each other on the quay to throw us ribbons and flowers, and shouts of farewell tinged with the salt taste of tears.

The shore draws further and further away and with it the bustle of the port. The horizon opens wide, and we are swallowed up in its vastness.

We land at Pusan in Korea, where we are packed into a train heading north. Towards dusk on the third day the convoy comes to a halt, and we leap gleefully to the ground to stretch our legs and empty our bladders. I whistle as I relieve myself, watching birds wheeling in the sky overhead. Suddenly I hear a stifled cry and I can see men running away into the woods. Tadayuki, fresh from the military academy, is lying stretched out on the ground ten paces away from me. The blood springs from his neck in a continuous stream, but his eyes are still

1 'Mother', in respectful Japanese.

open. Back in the train I cannot stop thinking about his young face twisted into a rictus of astonishment.

Astonishment. Is that all there is to dying?

The train arrives at a Manchurian station in the middle of the night. The frost-covered ground twinkles under the street lamps, and in the distance dogs are howling.

3

COUSIN LU taught me to play go when I was four years old and he was twice my age. The long hours of meditation, contemplating the chequered board, were a torment, but the will to win kept me there.

Ten years later Lu was considered an exceptional player, so famous for his talents that the Emperor of independent Manchuria[1] received him at his court in the new capital.[2] He never thanked me for propelling him to this glory: I am his shadow, his secret, his best opponent.

At twenty, Lu is already an old man, and the hair that falls over his brow is white. He walks with his back hunched over and his hands crossed, taking small steps. A

1 Pu-Yi, the last Emperor of China. He abdicated when the Chinese Republic was created in 1912. In 1932, with Japanese help, he fled from Tian Jing, where he had been living under guard. In order to legalise their occupation of northern China since 18th September 1931, the Japanese then put him on the throne of Manchuria and proclaimed its independence in March 1932.
2 Xin Jing, the capital of independent Manchuria, which is now the town of Chang Chun.

few pubescent hairs have appeared on his chin, a baby-beard on a centenarian.

A week ago I received a letter from him.

'I am coming for you, my little cousin. I have decided to talk to you about our future . . .'

The rest of the letter is an illegible confession: my painfully discreet cousin must have dipped his pen in very weak ink because his cursive ideograms are strung out between the watermarks like white storks flying in the mist. Endless and indecipherable, his letter written on a long sheet of rice paper undid me.

4

IT IS snowing so heavily that we have to stop training. Trapped by the frost, the cold and the wind, we spend our days playing cards in our rooms.

Apparently the Chinese who live out in the country in northern Manchuria never wash, and they ward off the cold by coating themselves in fish fat. As a result of our protests, a bathhouse has been built in our barracks, and officers and soldiers alike queue up outside it. Inside the bathhouse, through the haze of steam, the walls can be seen trickling with condensation. In the doorway, furious molten snow boils in a huge vat. Each man draws off his ration in a cracked enamel bucket.

I undress and wash myself with a towel dampened in this cloudy liquid. Not far away the officers have formed a circle, and as they scrub each other's backs, they discuss the latest news. As I go over to them, I recognise the man speaking: it is Captain Mori, one of the veterans who fought for Manchurian independence.

This morning's newspaper tells us that Major Zhang Xueliang has taken Chiang Kai-shek hostage in the town of Xian[1], where he and his exiled army have sought refuge for six years. In exchange for the generalissimo's freedom, Zhang Xueliang has demanded that the Kuomintang be reconciled with the Communist Party to reconquer Manchuria.

'Zhang Xueliang is unworthy of his good name and he's an inveterate womaniser,' Captain Mori says dismissively. 'The very day after 18th September 1931,[2] when our army had surrounded the town of Shen Yang where he had his headquarters, the degenerate weakling fled without even attempting to resist us. As for Chiang Kai-shek, he's a professional liar. He won't keep his promises. He'll welcome the Communists with open arms, the better to throttle them.'

'No Chinese army can take us on,' threw in one of the officers who was having his back energetically scrubbed by his orderly. 'The civil war ruined China. One day, we'll annex its entire territory, as we did with Korea.[3] You'll see, our army will go all the way down the railway that runs from northern China to the south. In three days we'll take Peking, and six days later we'll be marching through the streets of Nanking; eight days after that we'll be sleeping in Hong Kong, and that will open up the doors to South-East Asia.'

1 On 12th December 1936 Zhang Xueliang took Chiang Kai-shek hostage. He freed him on 25th December and accompanied him back to Nanking, where the Kuomintang – the popular democratic party in China – was based. As they stepped off the aeroplane, Chiang broke their agreement and imprisoned Zhang for some fifty years.
2 On 18th September 1931 the Japanese army defeated Zhang Xueliang's troops and took over Manchuria.
3 From 1905 to 1910 Japan succeeded in driving Russian and Chinese forces out of Korea, then it colonised the peninsula, enforcing the use of the Japanese language and instigating a policy of cultural assimilation.

Their comments serve to confirm various rumours, already rife in Japan, at the heart of our infantry. Despite our government's reticence, our conquest of China becomes more inevitable every day.

That evening I go to sleep relaxed, and happy to be clean.

I am roused from sleep by a rustling of clothes: I am sleeping in my own room, and Father is sitting in the next room, wrapped in his dark-blue cotton *yukata*. Mother is walking up and down, the bottom of her lavender-grey kimono opening and closing over a pale-pink under-kimono. She has the face of a young woman; there is not a single wrinkle round her almond-shaped eyes. A smell of springtime wafts around her – it's the perfume Father had sent from Paris!

I suddenly remember that she has not touched that bottle of perfume since Father died.

My dream disappears, leaving only pain and nostalgia.

5

COUSIN LU is becoming more and more stooped. He tries to behave with nonchalance, indifference, but those dark unsettling eyes peer out of his emaciated face, watching my every move. When I look into his eyes and ask him, 'What's the matter, Cousin Lu?', he says nothing.

I challenge him to a game of go. He turns pale and fidgets on his chair; his every move betrays his volatile mood. The territory he is trying to defend on the board is either too cramped or too sprawling, and his genius is reduced to a few strange and ineffectual moves. I can tell that he has again been reading ancient tracts on go; he gets them from his neighbour, an antique dealer, and a forger of the first order. I even wonder whether, after reading so many of these manuscripts, which are said to have sacred origins and are filled with Taoist mysteries and tragic anecdotes, my cousin is going to end up succumbing to madness, as players used to in the past.

'My cousin,' I say when, instead of thinking about his position, he is staring at my plait and daydreaming, 'what's happened to you?'

Lu flushes immediately as if I have found out his secret. He gives a little cough and looks like a doddering old man.

'What have you learned from your books, my cousin?' I taunt him impatiently. 'The secret of immortality? You look more and more like those dithering old alchemists who think they hold the secret of purple cinnabar.'

He isn't listening to me. He isn't looking at me either, but at his own last letter to me, which I have left on the table. Ever since he arrived he has been waiting for my reply to his illegible demands. I am determined not to breathe a word.

He goes home to the capital, full of flu, a broken man. I go to the station with him, and as I watch the train disappearing into the swirling snow I have a strange feeling of relief.

6

AT LAST, my first mission!
    Our detachment has received orders to track
down a group of terrorists who are challenging our
authority on the ground in Manchuria. Disguised as
Japanese soldiers, they attacked a military reserve and
stole arms and munitions.

For four days we follow a river locked under ice, with
the wind against us and the fallen snow swirling round
our knees. Despite my new coat, the cold slices through
me more sharply than a sabre, and I can no longer feel
my hands or feet. The marching has drained my head of
all thought. Laden like an ox and with my head tucked
down inside the collar of my uniform, I ruminate on the
hope that I will soon be able to warm myself by a camp
fire.

As we reach the foot of a hill, gunshots ring out. Just in
front of me several soldiers are hit and fall to the ground.
We are trapped! From their positions up above, the
enemy can shoot down on us and we cannot return their
fire. A sharp pain twists my gut – I'm wounded! I'm
dying! I feel tentatively with my hand: no wound at all,

just a cramp produced by fear – a discovery that covers me in shame. I look up and wipe the snow that has stuck to my eyes, and I can see that our more experienced soldiers have leaped down onto the frozen river, where they are sheltering behind the banks and returning fire. I leap to my feet and start to run. I could be hit a thousand times, but in war the difference between life and death depends on a mysterious game of chance.

Our machine guns open fire and, covered by their powerful barrage, we make our assault. To make up for my earlier cowardice, I launch myself into battle at the head of the platoon, brandishing my sabre.

I have been brought up in a world dominated by honour. I have known neither crime, poverty nor betrayal, and here I taste hatred for the first time: it is sublime, like a thirst for justice and revenge.

The sky is so charged with snow that it is threatening to collapse. The gunmen are sheltering behind huge boulders, but the smoke rising from their weapons gives away their position. I throw two grenades and when they explode, legs, arms and shreds of flesh fly out from a whirl of snow and flames. I scream with triumphant pleasure at this hellish sight and, leaping towards a survivor who is taking aim at me, I strike him with my sabre. His head rolls in the snow.

At last I can look my ancestors in the face. By handing their blade down to me they also bequeathed me their courage. I have not sullied their name.

The battle leaves us in a trance-like state. Stimulated by the blood, we whip our prisoners to break them down, but the Chinese are harder than granite, and they do not falter. We weary of the game and kill them: two bullets in the head.

Night falls and, fearing there may be other traps ahead, we decide to set up camp where we are. Our wounded groan in the dark, a dialogue of moans, and then silence. Their lips are frozen by the cold. They will not survive.

We gather up the bodies of the men we have lost, but the ground is so hard that we cannot even dig a ditch. Tomorrow the whole site will be picked clean by starving animals.

We wrap ourselves in anything we can find: dead men's clothes, abandoned blankets, tree branches, snow. We huddle together like sheep, and wait.

Eventually I fall asleep, savouring the melancholy pleasures of victory. I wake with a start to a muffled sound: the wolves could not wait for us to withdraw; they are already devouring the bodies.

7

COUSIN LU is coming back for New Year.

At the fair at the Temple of the White Horse we lose sight of our friends in the crowd and find ourselves alone together. He begs me to walk more slowly, and takes my hand. I snatch it back in disgust and start running, eager to get back to the others, but he keeps following me like a shadow, pleading with me to stop. I lose my temper and insist that we go back home immediately. But he pretends not to hear me and stands there blocking my way, under the sloping roof of a pavilion with icicles hanging down above our heads.

His eyes are gleaming, his cheeks are so frozen by the cold that they look like two pieces of dark-red cloth that have been cut out and stuck onto his ashen face. A thick layer of frost shimmers between his eyebrows and his fox-fur hat. I find his pathetic expression repulsive and I slip away, but he races after me and suggests that we go and see the lanterns sculpted in ice. I run all the faster. Lu strides on behind me and begs me to listen, his voice shaking and giving way to tears. I block my ears, but I am still haunted by his choked voice.

'What do you think about my letter?' he cries.

At this I stop, furious.

Intimidated, he does not dare come closer.

'Have you read it?' he goes on.

I give an unpleasant laugh.

'I tore it up,' I say, turning my back on him. He throws himself at me and crushes me in his arms.

'Listen to me!'

I push him away and say, 'Cousin Lu, let's play a game of go. If you win, I accept everything you propose. If you lose, we won't see each other again.'

8

THE TERRORISTS keep slipping through our fingers, and we celebrated New Year among the wolves and the foxes.

Today's snow is covering the snow that fell yesterday. We will pursue this enemy until he runs out of stores and ammunition.

How to describe the harshness of winter in northern China? Here the wind howls and trees are split in two by the weight of the ice. The fir trees look like funeral monuments daubed in black and white paint. Occasionally a fallow deer appears furtively, looks at us in amazement, then bolts.

We march on. It is such hard work that after an hour we are failing in the heat. We barely have time to catch our breath before the cold steals back inside our coats and freezes our limbs.

The enemy is cunning and knows the terrain well; he attacks when we least expect it, then withdraws. Despite our losses, we carry on, we persevere in this battle of endurance.

Whoever can stand up to exhaustion will come out of this hunt victorious.

9

THE GAME begins at dawn before the sun is really up, in a corner of the living room. His eyes are bloodshot, his hair unbrushed, he drinks cup after cup of tea to keep himself awake and he heaves great sighs. This morning, having spent two days visiting friends to offer them their good wishes for the New Year, my parents have dressed in traditional garments and are at home to receive guests. We take refuge in my room in a vain attempt to escape the greetings. People keep coming to find us: for some, we have to kneel down to wish them a good year and good fortune; for others, a brief bow will do. Adults are always hungry for compliments, and when we have flattered them, they slip us some money in a red envelope and invariably say, 'Run along, children, and buy yourself some sweets.'

Back at the go-board, Lu throws his envelopes onto the table scornfully. To annoy him, I open mine and count the notes, commenting on them as I do so.

'Stop it,' he says. 'You're not a child any more.'

I pull a face.

'You're going to be sixteen,' he mutters, exasperated. 'That's when women get married and have children.'

'Do you think you're going to marry me then?' I ask, bursting out laughing.

He goes quiet.

At noon there are so many drums and trumpets and firecrackers that the earth shakes. Through the windows I can see over the walls to where men and women dressed in red are dancing on stilts, weaving past each other in the sky, up between the trees.

Lu blocks his ears, but I find that the popular music heightens my concentration rather than distracting me. The winter light, tinted by the bright colours in the street, plays on the go-board. All these festivities cut me off from the rest of the world. My loneliness is like a bolt of crimson silk stowed in the bottom of a wooden chest.

After lunch my cousin drifts off into some vague meditation. He wipes a few stray tears from the corners of his eyes. I can no longer play the fool, so I say nothing. A silence as heavy as a plate of cold, unsalted noodles descends on the go-board.

My cousin is uneasy; he rests his head on his hand and keeps sighing. Towards seven in the evening he makes a mistake, and later in the evening, before the game is even finished, I point out that he has already lost and that he must stick to our agreement.

He pushes back his chair and stands up.

The following morning I am told that he has left. His train is at nine o'clock, so I still have time to catch him up. At the station he seems to be waiting for me to show some remorse. Whatever he hopes, I will never beg him for anything – it would only encourage him in his stupid ideas. He has offended me and he must submit himself to the punishment. Later I will write to him, I will call him back to me when his impure thoughts have given way to the humility of the defeated.

10

OUR PLATOON has surrounded a village shrouded in snow. The occupants were warned that we were coming, and men, women and children have fled, leaving just a few old people huddled in their tiny houses, which look all the more dismal with their scanty New Year decorations.

We round them up in the middle of the village. They have hardly any clothes, but they hide their skeletal bodies under darned old blankets, and their inane expressions under their fur hats. They shiver and moan, seeking to make us feel sorry for them. Try as I might to talk to them in Mandarin, they do not understand a word and answer in some unintelligible dialect. Exasperated, I threaten them with my pistol, and three of them throw themselves at my feet, clutching my legs and pleading their innocence in perfect Mandarin. Horrified, I try to break away from them by beating them back with the butt of my rifle, but they cling to me all the harder and beat their heads against the tops of my thighs.

My obvious embarrassment makes the soldiers laugh.

'Come and help me, you idiot!' I call to one of them.

His laughter turns to a grimace of resentment and, in one swift movement, he takes his rifle from his shoulder and plunges the bayonet into the leg of one of the old men.

The wounded man rolls on the ground, howling in pain, and his two terrified companions fall away from me. Having recovered from the initial shock, I yell at the soldier, 'You bloody fool, you could have injured me.'

Another burst of laughter from the spectators.

The cruelty displayed by our troops is fed by our harsh upbringing: slapping, punching and insults are used daily as reprimands for children. As a way of cultivating submission and humility in the army, officers beat the lower ranking officers and soldiers until they bleed, or they slash their cheeks with specially sharpened bamboo rulers.

I find it repulsive to torture innocent people, and I feel sorry for these Chinese peasants who live in ignorance, poverty and squalor. They are peace-loving, and they would not mind whether they had to obey a Manchurian emperor, a Chinese war-lord or a Japanese emperor so long as their bellies were filled every day.

I order my soldiers to bandage the wounded man and to take the threesome back to their homes. We search their houses and take all their provisions, down to the last pinch of flour. I promise to return everything if they tell us where the terrorists are hiding.

The next day, before dawn, someone comes to wake us.

Hunger has loosened his tongue. We do not wait for the sun to rise before setting off into the snowstorm.

11

TEN DAYS later I receive a letter from Lu. He tells me he has obtained a passport for the inner territories,[1] and that by the time I read his letter he will have left for Peking. I feel strangely sad as I decipher his words. I go to the Square of a Thousand Winds where the players, unperturbed, abandon themselves to their own particular passion.

As a little girl I used to follow my cousin wherever he played. Once he was so consumed with fever that he passed out on the go-board, and I won the tournament for him, a victory that made me the only woman to be admitted into the exclusive society for true enthusiasts.

Years have passed and now I am anxiously watching the twilight of my childhood, quietly sinking, never to rise again.

Lu doesn't understand me. He wants me to join him in

1 As Manchuria is often called 'the country outside the Great Wall', the areas inside the Great Wall are also known as the 'inner territories'. In 1932, when Manchuria became independent, the Japanese instituted a system of passports so that they had more control over movements between the zone that was under their influence and the rest of China.

the adult world, but he doesn't realise that I think it is a sad place full of vanity, and it frightens me.

12

NEW ORDERS have reached us. We have to burn the stores in all the villages so that the terrorists have no sources of supplies.

When we have ransacked the village, it seems as sad and gloomy as a grave. The howling wind mingles with weeping as the peasants prostrate themselves before the ochre flames and black smoke.

The snow-clad forest has cut us off from the outside world for three months now. There is more and more violence among my men, who spend their time getting drunk and quarrelling. The white, the grey, the reflected light and the endless marching are all slowly driving us mad. The day before yesterday a corporal took all his clothes off and fled. He was found unconscious in a ravine, and now we have to tie him up and pull him along with a rope round his neck. Lulled by his curses and his piercing laughter, I realise that many of the same ideas are spinning round and round in my own head like a refrain.

While we wait to be consumed by madness, we have

to keep on advancing, through the snow, towards the
snow.

13

I AM bored at my all-girls school.

Our national education system churns out laughably affected 'young ladies', and one day my classmates will be irreproachable society women. The prettiest of them is called Huong and her eyebrows are so carefully plucked that they form two crescent moons above her eyes. She draws them together, screws them up, smooths them out again. Her feigned joy and her mannered laugh will never completely disguise the uneasiness of puberty.

The ugliest of them, although she does in fact have the longest hair in the class, is called Zhou. Her thankless face means she is free to judge things with as much scorn and bitterness as she pleases, and that is her charm. Apparently her mother, a woman built like a Mongol wrestler and the niece of a very high-ranking officer, has lost no time throwing her weight about in the capital.

Between lessons the girls talk about film stars, dresses, jewellery, marriage and the Empress's secret affairs. No one reads any new literature with its venomous attacks on our crumbling society; no one mentions the latest political events, which are more devastating every day.

Romantic novels are handed from one girl to the next to solicit their easy tears. Independent Manchuria cuts us off from the rest of China. It is like a silk factory, producing something so soft and wonderful, but the silkworms themselves die in a boiling bath once they have woven their delicate cocoons.

After lessons, I go to the Square of a Thousand Winds. Everything about the game of go propels me towards a world where things move and evolve. The constantly changing faces help me to forget the platitudes of my everyday life.

The girls at school have nicknamed me the 'foreigner'. To them, my passion for go is like some exotic madness. The players themselves prefer to be indulgent, which is to their credit, so they tolerate my childishly extravagant enthusiasm.

Twenty years ago, after he was married, Father persuaded Grandfather to send him to England to study. When he returned a year later, Father was Westernised and flouted tradition: he entrusted my sister Moon Pearl to his mother and took his wife along with him to share his troubled life in the West. This caused a great scandal in Peking, where both families were living. Maternal Grandfather, a retired court dignitary, broke off relations with Paternal Grandfather, who still held an honourable position there. I was born in the mists of London, and the evils of this displaced birth were soon manifested in the wilfulness of my troubled soul. Sadly, I don't have any memories of my early childhood. When the Empire collapsed, the two old men were reconciled, united in their loathing of the republicans, and they died within days of each other. My parents came back for the period of mourning and they obeyed my grandmother's orders by leaving Peking and coming here, where my ancestors had built their hunting lodge.

Grandmother, who dreamed of peace, died the day after the war of 18th September 1931. When Chinese soldiers took refuge in our town five days after their defeat, they broke our door down, occupied the house and installed their wounded in it.

The Japanese besieged us, and the shelling went on for three days. A bomb exploded on our house and a great deal of our precious furniture served to feed the triumphant flames. The Chinese army capitulated and we never saw the soldiers again. According to the rumours, 3,000 men were taken outside the town and shot.

After Grandmother died, our life gradually resumed its normal course. The Japanese appointed a new mayor, the barricades disappeared, enemy flags flew above the roofs, Japanese shops opened and, in restaurants, the traditional white-cotton door blind was replaced with one printed with Japanese writing. Japanese women with their tall, glossy, lacquered chignons walked along our streets. Constrained by their narrow kimonos, they took tiny little footsteps, clacking their clogs on the cobblestones.

We had to build a new house, but inflation had made us poor. Mother dismissed her chambermaids, and kept only the cook and one maid. The ruined aristocracy was replaced by the nouveaux riches, who brought a sort of pompous gaiety to the town. Hotels, luxurious shops and elegant restaurants opened – the avenues of our town had never been so prosperous.

My parents each found their own way of escaping reality: Father toiled over the translation of an anthology of English poetry; Mother busied herself copying out his manuscript, replacing his over-hurried words with her careful calligraphy.

Mother sealed her overseas memories in a chest. When she is away I take the opportunity to steal the key, which she keeps in a vase. Photographs, clothes, letters and printed fabrics in extraordinary designs that exude a bewitching smell . . . not musk, or cedar, or sandalwood; not the flowers we have in our garden, the trees we have in our towns; but a perfume that transports me to another world.

Dreaming only deepens my sadness.

14

A T LAST! After a month of arduous tracking through the mountains, we have trapped the terrorists. We have cornered them on the edge of a precipice, and they will only be able to escape if they can fly.

We finished the bulk of our provisions a long time ago, and while we waited for new supplies, we shared what little we had. We can each count on the fingers of one hand the biscuits that have been handed out, and which we eat with mouthfuls of snow.

Yesterday at noon, with all our ammunition spent, we took the decision to charge straight on at the Chinese with fixed bayonets.

This morning a strange feeling of calm has settled on the mountain. There is not a breath of wind and only the cries of pheasants stand out against the silence. I am writing my will – the words of farewell calm my nerves.

I slowly draw the sabre from its sheath, and wipe the blade with my handkerchief. This steel forged at the beginning of the sixteenth century has never looked so shiny, so bright. In the past it has sliced off countless heads in the service of my ancestors. Today it is a mirror, reflecting the menacing purity of death.

Suddenly a bugle sounds. I bound out of the trench and hurl myself towards the enemy with a fierce war-cry. Up on the mountaintop nothing moves: not one shadow, not a single man. The terrorists have flown away! A soldier is waving to us from the edge of the precipice. About a hundred metres below, the snow is dotted with bodies. The gunmen must have thrown down their weapons, their dead and their wounded, before hurling themselves over the edge. Now I understand why at about midday yesterday, after a violent exchange of fire, their guns fell silent.

The ammunition in both camps ran out at the same time, but neither knew of the other's plight. We were all on the verge of collapse.

The Japanese had chosen to be glorious in their action, and the Chinese in their deaths. The pathetic heroism of their collective suicide is tainted by a sad irony: killing yourself too soon is a shameful form of surrender. The Chinese civilisation is several thousand years old and has produced an infinite number of philosophers, thinkers and poets. But not one of them has grasped the irreplaceable energy of death.

Our more modest civilisation is the only one that has grappled with this essential truth: to act is to die; to die is to act.

15

ONE CUSTOM that we have imported from the West is that the New Year marks the beginning of the season for parties.

My sister dresses me in one of her European dresses, then she parts my hair on one side and waxes it thoroughly before opening her make-up box. In just one hour I have become unrecognisable even to myself. My face is as white as over-soaped linen, my eyelids are darker than a moth's wings, and the fluttering false eyelashes make me look winsomely tearful.

On the square in front of the town hall the garlands are vying for attention with the stars. Carriages and cars glide over the snow and spew out 'gentlemen' fingering gold-handled canes, and women in furs, with curled hair and cigarettes at the end of ivory filters held nonchalantly between their lips.

A wood of fir trees sparkling in the snow lies between the Imperial Hotel and the rest of the world. A pathway swept clear at the beginning of the evening zigzags between the shadows and the wavering torchlight. The hotel porters in their red capes are clearly silhouetted against the glassy clarity of the windows.

A revolving door projects me into a huge room, where red lacquered columns reach up towards a domed ceiling hung with crystal chandeliers like bouquets of fireworks. Mountains, forests and seas undulate around the walls, and the sun contemplates the moon as storks fly off towards the clouds.

My sister drags me over to a table and orders me a *café au lait*, a fashionable sort of drink to have in a place like this. The band accompanies a singer in a sequinned dress that gleams as her body moves like a charmed snake, while her milky-white throat produces a moody, plaintive voice.

Soon my brother-in-law asks my sister to dance and they head for the dance floor. Looking into each other's eyes and holding hands, they look beautiful and elegant as they move rhythmically backwards and forwards, round and round. The music speeds up and my sister smiles and flushes as she lets herself be carried away by it. When the waltz ends amid general applause, my brother-in-law kisses her gently on the shoulder and I feel a constriction grip my heart: who could guess how much he makes her suffer?

I look round the tables and see Huong, who must have been watching me for a while. My classmate greets me with a little nod, and I would like to be swallowed up by the ground to hide my horrible make-up. What will she tell them tomorrow? I'm going to be a laughing stock.

As I struggle with my embarrassment, she waves to me, inviting me over to her table. I get up slowly and, as I reach her, I can see the thick powder on her cheeks. She is wearing a completely backless dress, and I find this extravagance reassuring. I am not the only one who looks like a caricature.

A man offers me his place and goes to find a chair. Huong introduces me to her friends, who seem a lot older. She is very friendly towards me and for the first time I can see how gracious her carefully chosen words are. Now that any animosity between us has evaporated, I can admit to her how hostile I feel towards this stuffy, hypocritical society.

She looks at me for a long time and then raises her glass towards me.

'You must drink. Otherwise you'll always be an outsider.'

The champagne fizzes in my throat and makes me cough. I am won over by the gaiety of the evening and, encouraged by Huong, I dare to look up and meet male eyes. A man asks me to dance and I feel like a bear walking beside him. When I come back to Huong, her hysterical laughter is contagious: this girl I have never liked is suddenly my accomplice, my friend.

As we leave the hotel, still drunk, I insist that we go back to the car on foot. My sister scolds me, but it isn't long before the idea appeals to her: I need to sober up before we get home.

One shadow stands out against the dark mass of the woods: a naked body with its arms across its belly, staring up at the sky.

Last summer the Resistance Movement attacked enemy convoys, so the Japanese burned all the fields along the railway line. Ever since, hordes of ruined peasants wander up and down our streets, begging for a few grains of rice. A corpse can no longer defend itself: the other beggars have taken all this man's clothes.

WHAT A pleasure it is receiving my first letters! Venerable Mother gives me a detailed account of the New Year festivities, and I learn from Little Sister one detail that she preferred to keep to herself: since I left, Mother goes to the temple every day and prays for hours on end. On the other hand, Little Sister has had a dream that Buddha has taken me into his protection.

Little Brother's letter is elliptical – as usual, this doctor of classical letters is economical with his words and his emotions. He concedes that, at the moment, the homeland needs soldiers more than it needs writers. I read his words with tears in my eyes – his message is clear, he is asking my forgiveness for misunderstanding me for so long.

As an adolescent, after Father's death, I felt such an anguished love for my brother that I embarked on a peculiarly intense relationship with him, like that between a father and son, a trainer and an athlete or an officer and a soldier. So that he would live up to my fierce expectations, I forced him to learn the games at which I excelled. Little Brother pretended to obey me and patiently waited for his opportunity to rebel.

The day came. It's nature's way: there comes a time when the eldest loses his power over his siblings. When he was sixteen Little Brother was as tall as me, he had become a young man, he had a solid bone structure and impressive muscles. One day he solemnly challenged me in the kendo club. The next moment I was hit right across the face by a wooden sabre, such a powerful blow that I staggered. When I regained my balance, the victor bowed and thanked me for accepting the challenge. He took off his mask: his face was gleaming with sweat and glowing with secret delight. He bowed a respectful goodbye and left the *dojo* still wearing his kendo clothes.

Later, the boy said he wanted to be a writer, and he enrolled at the University of Tokyo. Since then our paths have gone their separate ways. At university he spent so much time with left-wing students that he became aggressive and contemptuous. Influenced by anarchist authors, he took a hostile stance towards the military, accusing them of interfering in government affairs, and calling them 'assassins of liberty'.

I no longer had the time or the patience to set my brother straight. He had, anyway, taken to making himself scarce whenever I was at home. As far as I was concerned, Little Brother was lost, swept away on the great tide of red.

Why this change of heart now? Had he quarrelled with his friends? Who had revealed to him how vain Marxism was and how ridiculous their ideas of utopia?

I reply with a letter as brief as his: 'My brother, after my first battle the only thing I now worship is the sun, a star that represents death's constancy. Beware of the moon, which reflects our world of beauty. It waxes and wanes, it is treacherous and ephemeral. We will all die some day. Only our nation will live on. Thousands of generations of patriots will together create Japan's eternal greatness.'

17

A T MY age one friendship wipes out another, flaring up like a fire then dying down; they're never constant, but each glows fiercely.

By inviting Huong to have supper with my family I am opening up my universe to her. In her quilted blue Chinese dress, and with her hair in two plaits the good little schoolgirl wins my parents over. After supper, I offer her some tea and invite her to my room. She crosses the threshold as carefully as someone stepping into a dream.

To show her how magical this old room really is – it is one of the few to have escaped the bombing – I turn out the lamps and light the candles. Scrolls of calligraphy and paintings loom out of the darkness and gradually blend with the tinted frescos on the walls. There is a majestic set of shelves full of books at one end, and on my lacquered table little painted birds frolic among the leaves. Two pots of go-stones have pride of place on top of an old carved wardrobe, to watch over me at night. Huong picks up a manual about go and leafs through it. She takes one of the combs I collect, long and fine, made of polished silver and decorated with feathers. She fingers my pearls. A long silence falls between us.

Then she sits on the edge of the bed and opens her heart to me: she was born out in the country and she lost her mother when she was eight years old. Her father remarried and was completely crushed by his new wife's bulk and drive: she would set off every morning with a pipe in her mouth to oversee work in the fields. The stepmother hated Huong, and it was not long before the arrival of her twin stepbrothers deflected her father's affection. To them she was just a slut. As they grew up, the boys took pleasure in hurting her: they tormented her like two young cats toying with an injured sparrow. She was constantly insulted by her stepmother, who was peculiarly eloquent when it came to insults. Huong was exiled to a little maid's room and, at night, she would count the raindrops falling on the roof. They were innumerable, like the sorrows she had to endure.

When she was twelve she was sent to school: the stepmother was rid of the thorn in her side and Huong discovered freedom.

She was a passionate and determined child, and she shook off her accent and transformed herself into one of the young town girls. It didn't take her long to understand what made these city-dwellers tick, and she put these mechanisms to her own use. Thanks to a few coins slipped into the boarding housemistress's pocket and a couple of bottles of wine at the end of the year, she was given permission to go out whenever she liked. She shared a room with girls older than herself, and was initiated into the pleasures of champagne and chocolate and the waltz. By imitating them she learned to put on make-up, to lie about her age and to get herself invited to balls. Men came to fetch her in their cars, whispering sweet nothings to her and telling her how beautiful she was.

Since then, the holidays have become pure torture. Back there, the house is dark and damp, and the smell of the draught animals is disgusting. Her father spits on the floor, her stepmother shrieks at everyone, and her brothers – instead of sitting properly at the table – squat on their chairs so that they can guzzle their food all the more efficiently.

It is nearly night-time and I offer Huong my bed. She snuggles into it, next to the wall, and carries on talking until her words become muddled and her voice dwindles to a whisper.

I stay awake for a long time. My friend is seventeen, and her father is looking for a husband for her – that will bring an end to a party that has gone on for three years. Will she ever meet a man who can change her fate?

18

THERE ARE days when I suddenly have new strength and will, and I can look death in the face with a sense of peace and joy. Guided by my country's need, I fulfil the destiny of an imperial soldier with my eyes closed. But the path that a hero must tread is not as straight as we might imagine: it twists and turns through the harsh mountains of sacrifice.

This morning I wake up lying on my stomach on ground that has been burned dry by the sun. I snooze on in the warmth rising up from deep in the earth. My eyes are still heavy with sleep and it is a long time before I open them and become aware of a tombstone just centimetres from my face. I have been sleeping on my mother's tomb.

I stifle a cry of alarm and wake myself up properly this time. The winter sun is not yet up, and this room requisitioned from peasants is like a cave. My soldiers are snoring in the dark. Who can give me the key to my dream? How can I know whether it was a premonition? Could it be a message from my mother before she leaves this world? Who can I find to tell me – here and now, thousands of kilometres from Tokyo? Is Mother alive and well?

I have thought about my own death for so many years that it has become as light as a feather, but having never prepared myself for my mother's death, I will be unable to bear its weight.

It is impossible to reconcile family and fatherland: a soldier is a man who destroys his loved ones' happiness. If my life has been of any use, the nation owes that to one woman's sacrifice.

Feeling my way in the dark, I find a piece of paper and a pencil stub. I cannot even see what I am doing, but I write a short letter to Mother, telling her of my regret. I have neglected her for so long!

I fold it in four and slip it under my pillow. How many days do we still have to endure before we renew contact with the world?

H UONG MAKES a strange confession to me.
'My father is very rich, but I have to beg from him. He gets angry whenever I ask him for money, and he ends up giving me only half what I need, throwing it down onto the table at me.' Then she goes on, 'I'll marry an older man who'll know how to pamper me.'

A few days later she leads me to understand that she has fallen for someone.

'You see,' she says, 'a real man is different, not like the boys with their moustaches who lurk outside our school. He can guess what you're thinking, anticipate what will make you happy. When you're with a man, you're no longer a girl but a goddess, a sage, an ancient soul who has lived in every era, a wonder that he contemplates with all the intense curiosity of a new-born baby.'

Even though Huong has become my best friend, I never quite understand what she is saying. Her convoluted soul is divided between light and darkness, she is both blatant and discreet, and her life is full of mysteries despite everything she admits to me. This Monday morning she has come to school exhausted and on edge.

Although her hair is plaited, I can see evidence that it has been curled and then straightened. She is intoxicated with some joy that only she understands.

'The best demonstration of love a man can give,' she tells me, 'is his patience as he watches a virgin maturing.'

I flush and find I can't utter a word. She doesn't seem at all embarrassed to be talking about something so intimate, and yet there is a grandeur, a heroism to her indiscreet confessions. There is a realm of life that I haven't yet grasped. I feel like a blind person who has never seen the splendour of the sun.

'How can I get out of this darkness around us?' I ask Huong.

She pretends not to understand.

'How can I become a woman?'

She opens her eyes wide and cries, 'You're mad. Leave it as late as possible!'

20

Back to the civilised world.

The town of Ha Rebin is in the northern extremity of Manchuria, a strategic place in the Sino-Russian conflict. Our warships are challenging the Russian navy on the River Love, which is several kilometres wide.

When twilight falls on this noisy, bustling town, the domes of all the mosques, the crosses and virgins on the churches, and the sloping roofs of the Buddhist temples are all silhouetted against the bloodied brilliance of the sky. Russians, Jews, Japanese, Koreans, Chinese, English, Germans and Americans live side by side in this cosmopolitan metropolis. Each of these peoples has found a way of re-creating its own landscape and living according to its own culture.

Yesterday I slept among bales of straw, lulled by the howling wolves and the moaning wind. I drank melted snow. My uniform was burned, full of holes and ingrained with sweat and filth. Today I am in a clean uniform and back in a bed with a woollen blanket in a heated room. I am off to visit the prostitutes with a few of the other officers. I blow my savings by choosing a Japanese girl.

Masayo, a young prostitute originally from Toyama, pours me a drink. Her make-up is unremarkable, her perfume bland, her kimono garish and the way she handles the bottle is clumsy, but still she manages to dazzle me. When I catch hold of her hand, the touch of a woman's skin has the same effect on me as an electric shock. I pull her to me violently and she falls into my arms. I rip open her loosely tied kimono and tear her underwear. Two white breasts spring out.

The pink of her nipples is more than I can bear. After months of solitude, I want to expire in a woman's body. I knead her breasts with my hand and straddle her, despite her protests. My sex finds hers and I have scarcely penetrated her before a luxuriant pain sweeps over me and gently turns me inside out.

Back in the street, I walk with a spring in my step, both emptied and full of new energy. The prostitute has injected me with the human warmth that I had lost.

21

THE SQUARE in front of the town hall is seething with people, and with my basket over my arm I drag Moon Pearl through the crowds. She complains about being jostled, about the price of grain, about how little game there is for sale. She is unusually talkative and strangely jumpy as she criticises everything we buy. I am exasperated by her constant moaning, and I can't wait to be rid of her.

In the last three years her life has changed into a great river of despair. I so miss my bright, cheerful sister with her dark plaited hair tied with fiery coloured ribbons. She used to be constantly on the move, spinning round, sitting down only to get straight back up again. She persecuted us with that explosive laugh of hers.

Today a few wisps of wavy hair straggle from under her hood and float limply on her pale cheeks. Her hair has lost its shine, a metaphor for her entire being, dulled and subdued.

I shake her by the arm.

'Why don't you divorce him then!'

She stares at me, opening her beautiful slanting eyes wide. Tears stream over her face.

'He loved me, Little Sister . . . ! He swore I would be the only woman in his life . . . ! I don't think he's forgotten his promise. It's stronger than him . . . Yesterday evening I followed him . . . he went to the theatre with some loose woman, a depraved creature who let him fondle her in his theatre box . . .'

I don't know what to say to her. Our new customs have condemned polygamy, but this hasn't stopped men being fickle, or released women from their suffering. My parents are very enlightened in an age completely torn between tradition and modernity, they encouraged my sister to marry the man of her choice – a marriage of love that has caused pain and unhappiness.

People are glancing at us and turning to listen, but Moon Pearl is too convulsed by her tears to realise how ridiculous she looks. Luckily a rickshaw comes past; I stop it, put my sister on the seat and ask the man to take her home. She is so intoxicated by her pain that she doesn't even try to resist.

I carry on buying the things Mother has asked me to find. The local farmers and hunters come here every Sunday, travelling overnight to stand shivering outside the city gates, waiting for them to be opened. I finish my shopping as the sun reaches its zenith; the snow has melted this morning and there is an icy slush underfoot as I head for a tea-room. They have set up a stove by the door, so I sit down beside the stall and order an almond and hazelnut tea. The boy serves me quickly: a thin stream of scorching water flows from the spout of a giant kettle decorated with dragons, and lands in a bowl a good metre away. Behind me someone starts to sing:

'My village lies in the arms of the River Love,
On the edge of an ocean of pine trees
How can I forget its loveliness,
My mother, my sisters,
How can I abandon them to the mercy
Of the invaders?'

A shiver runs through the crowd: the song has been banned. Anyone who dares sing it risks being sent to prison. I see people looking round in astonishment with pale, anxious faces. Just ten paces from me the brave individual starts again, and he is soon joined by other voices. More and more people join in the chorus and the song spreads through the whole market.

Policemen blow whistles to sound the alarm. Shots are fired. Rallied by the gunfire, a peasant who had been crouching beside his basket of eggs gets to his feet, clutching a gun in his hand. Some distance away another takes rifles from on top of some straw bales and hands them out. These armed men head towards the town hall, jostling passers-by as they go. The tea-stall collapses, making a terrible noise, and I am carried away by the crowd.

People are crying, shouting and wailing in terror. It is no longer clear who is advancing towards the government guards and who is dropping back to try and escape. A human tide carries me towards the gates of the town hall where the gunfire is intensifying. I struggle, but the men's blood is up and they hardly notice me. I trip on a body and fall. My fumbling hands come across a cold, wet jacket: a policeman lies there stabbed, staring at me with his blank, upturned eyes. I get back to my feet, but one of the peasants brandishing his rifle jabs me with his elbow and I fall back onto the body. I scream in horror.

A young man leans over and offers me his hand. He heaves me up. He is a student with a swarthy complexion. He smiles at me.

'Come on,' he says. He gives a quick nod and another student appears, casts a contemptuous eye over me and takes hold of my other arm. They raise me up between the two of them as they forge a path through the crowd.

There are fierce, noisy battles in the streets, and the two students flee, dragging me with them. As if they already know which police positions have been attacked by the rebels, they avoid these sites of bloodshed and eventually come to a stop by the gates to an impressive property. One of them opens the door to reveal an abandoned garden where crocuses peep up through the snow. The house is European in style with half-moon archways and diamond-shaped window panes.

'This is Jing's house,' says the swarthy-faced student, indicating his friend. 'My name is Min.'

Min explains that the owner of this property, an aunt of Jing's, has moved to Nanking, and that Jing has willingly taken on the post of overseer. His deep, youthful voice sounds not unlike the man who was singing earlier.

'And you?'

I introduce myself and ask if I can use the telephone.

'The rebels have almost certainly cut the telephone lines,' Jing tells me rather impatiently, but when Min sees the look of despair on my face he offers to try for me.

The bare walls in the sitting room still bear marks where pictures must have hung, and the red lacquered floorboards are scratched and scored where furniture has been moved. In the library hundreds of books still stand in neat lines on the shelves, while others have been thrown haphazardly on the floor. The low tables are cluttered with full ashtrays, dirty cups and plates and crumpled newspapers. It looks as if a meeting was held here last night.

Min opens a door to reveal the bedroom and a bed draped in crimson silk dotted with chrysanthemums. He picks up the telephone on a side-table, but can't get a line.

'I'll take you home when everything's calmed down,' he says in his warm, friendly voice. 'You're safe here. Are you hungry? Come and help me make something to eat.'

While Min prepares the noodles, peels the vegetables and cuts up the meat, Jing sits on a stool by the window listening to the commotion outside. There are occasional gunshots, and with every shot a mocking smile appears on the corners of his lips. I don't know what will happen to my town, I think that these pseudo-peasants are members of the Resistance Movement against the Japanese army. The newspapers say they are bandits who pillage, burn, take citizens hostage and then use the ransom money to buy arms from the Russians. Anxious about my parents and about Moon Pearl lost in the streets in her rickshaw, I sit down, get back up again, pace up and down the room, leaf through books and then slump down onto a stool next to Jing.

Like him, I listen to every sound. Only Min seems to be calm, whistling an opera tune as he works. A delicious smell wafts over from the cooking-pot and it isn't long before Min proudly presents me with a bowl of noodles with beef and sweet-and-sour cabbage. He hands me a pair of chopsticks.

That is when I remember that they are waiting for me at home to celebrate my sixteenth birthday.

22

A<small>T HA REBIN</small> the sunlight pierces the eyes.
In springtime, there is a constant thundering as the great debris of ice is buffeted, thrown up and submerged in the foaming torrents of the River Love.

A rich salesman has just set up a lottery stand in the town centre, and he is announcing the results of the draw from a raised platform. Beggars with hardly a shred of clothing shiver beside men in thick furs. The whole town is here, the thieves and the thankless, the military and the students, the rich housewives and the prostitutes, all waiting impatiently. The long-awaited announcement is greeted with groans of despair and some cries of joy from the crowd. Fights break out, husbands beat their wives because they changed their numbers, and those who have just gambled their last few coins are threatening to commit suicide. There are also creditors claiming their dues, and winners who can no longer find their tickets.

I have never known a place where the wealthy are so conscious of their riches while the poor struggle so desperately against destitution. The lack of purpose in this population confirms my opinion: the Chinese Empire has sunk irretrievably into chaos. This ancient civilisation has imploded under the reign of the Manchurians, who refused openness, science and modernisation. Today, as the chosen prey of the Western powers, it survives by relinquishing land and autonomy. Only the Japanese, who have inherited a pure, unhybridised version of Chinese culture,[1] have made it their vocation to liberate the Empire from the European yoke. We will give her people back their peace and dignity.

We are their saviours.

---

1 From the sixth century Buddhism and Chinese culture infiltrated the Yamato Imperial court of Japan. In 604 Prince Shotoku sent an official embassy to the court of Tchang An (now Xiang) in China. In 645 the Yamato court decided to turn Japan into a copy of Tang China, and Japanese calligraphy adopted Chinese ideograms. The political problems within the Tang court, and the Tatar invasion, persuaded the Japanese to withdraw their embassy in 838. From then on Japanese culture has evolved independently from that on the Chinese mainland.

23

JING HAS been to find out what is going on and he tells us that rebels have occupied the town hall and thrown the mayor's body over the balcony. In the space of a few hours, hatred has spread through the town, and the people, stirred up by the bloodshed, are massacring collaborators and Japanese immigrants. Some Chinese soldiers who were enrolled into the Manchurian army have turned against the Japanese and are now surrounding the enemy division in their barracks.

Min puts a ladder up against the wall and we climb onto the roof. The town spreads out before our eyes, an infinity of serried rooftops, grey fish scales glinting silver. Sinuous roads cut deep, dark furrows. The naked plane trees spell out their arid calligraphy, and columns of black smoke rise from the town centre, piercing the violet and yellow sky where thousands of sparrows circle in panic.

We can hear shots among the shouting, the cheering and the celebratory drumming. Some areas look deserted and mournful, others look jubilant and full of life. In the distance the ramparts of the town meander through a thick mist.

Will they be strong enough to withstand the Japanese reinforcements?

24

D URING OUR brief, statutory polite conversation I
discover that Madame Violette, Masayo's employer,
is also originally from Tokyo. Meeting compatriots on
foreign soil produces a melancholy happiness and turns
complete strangers into close friends. Within moments
she is offering me some *sake* and bombarding me with
questions about my life. I then ask her about her family,
and she says that her husband and children were killed in
the earthquake. From the sleeve of her kimono she
produces a tiny child's sandal, the only reminder she has
of her son. Fourteen years have elapsed and I have
managed to banish the images of that seismic disaster to
the furthest recesses of my memory, but Madame
Violette's tears bring back those scenes of devastation.

Catastrophe struck at noon. The bells ringing for the
end of morning lessons had only just begun to sound
when chairs suddenly overturned around us and sticks of
chalk flew through the air. Thinking this was some
practical joke set up by my classmates, I started laughing
and clapping, but then the blackboard came crashing
down with a thud, injuring several children as it

shattered. The walls shook and our heavy wooden work tables began gliding from one side of the room to the other. One boy got trapped under the furniture and screamed in terror. We had only just extricated him when a hail of plaster pelted down on us.

Our teacher, also covered in the white powder, ran to the window, opened it, and ordered us to jump. I was the first to throw myself out into the void: our classroom was on the second floor and I landed unharmed on my hands and feet in the grass below. Others followed me. Some of the boys jumping from the floors above injured themselves and we dragged them by the shoulders towards the garden. The whole façade of the building quivered. The three entrance doors spewed a constant stream of pupils who had fought their way to the doors bare-headed, with torn uniforms and bloodied shirts. Suddenly the central building caved in on itself in one slow, irresistible descent, heaving with it the wings on either side.

The garden was seething with people screaming, groaning, running and crawling as the ground rippled beneath them. The paved paths that I had trodden so many times twisted like lengths of ribbon, and the trees we clung to arched and teetered before hurling us to the ground. We tried with no more success to cling to the grass and shrubs. A strange roaring sound rose from the centre of the earth, and a torrent of rock and stone, the harsh, dry sound of torn silk.

When the tremors stopped, the staff and prefects grouped us together and made us sit in a circle on the sports ground. They told us not to move, and started to tend the injured and count the missing. I caught a glimpse of my younger brother in the distance and the joy of seeing him brought tears to my eyes. Somewhere in the crowd a boy was wailing and soon everyone had joined him.

We were forbidden to go anywhere near the rubble to look for survivors: we had to be patient and wait for the emergency services, but at five o'clock in the afternoon still no one had come. By then the wind was stronger and, when flames flickereed up from a building, suffocating billows of black smoke were buffeted and spread by the typhoon. Making the most of the confusion, I hopped over a collapsed wall and ran away along the street.

The scenes that greeted me came straight from hell. Tokyo had disappeared. Although some buildings were still standing, scarcely holding each other up, the roads had been submerged under a thick layer of bricks, wood and glass. People looked for their loved ones, helplessly calling their names. One madman wandered through the ruins laughing. Three nuns were crouched over the remains of a church, digging with their bare hands in the hope of finding a living soul.

Houses were burning and, with the aid of the wind, the fires spread. It was six o'clock in the evening and the dark ash whirling through the sky made the night close in. What happened next is confused in my memory. I can see myself feeling my way through this suffocating darkness, my path scattered with masonry, with people trying to flee the danger and with dead bodies. I do not remember how I managed to reach our doorstep. I saw my mother sitting on a tree trunk, looking at the few things she had been able to save, with Little Sister at her feet, clinging to her legs. The sound of my footsteps woke her from her dazed silence and she looked up sharply. From the way she threw herself at me I could tell some great sadness was going to carve its way into me like an arrowhead.

'Father has just left us.'

I watched over my father's battered corpse all night. His face was at peace, as if he were contemplating paradise, and his hands were as icy-cold as the underworld. From time to time I would get up and walk to the end of the garden, from where we could see the whole city at a glance: Tokyo was burning, a vast funeral pyre.

According to legend, Japan is an island floating on the back of a catfish, and the fish's movements cause the earthquakes. I tried to picture this aquatic monster. The pain I felt was like a fever. I became delirious. Unable to kill the god responsible for this, we had to attack the continent. China, an infinite and stable land, was within our grasp – that was where we would guarantee our children's safe future.

When Masayo arrives, I am torn away from a conversation that was becoming unbearably painful. She bows to the ground in front of her employer, who is weeping silently, then drags me by the sleeve and leads me up to her room.

25

THE RESISTANCE partisans withdrew into the mountains before nightfall, and were followed by those soldiers who had rebelled. In the space of an evening the town's patriotic fever has dropped.

The very next morning Japanese patrols are parading through the streets. A provisional government has been constituted; they are noisily tracking down and dealing with the rioters. If they fail to find any true rebels, they vent their anger on thieves and beggars.

The new mayor decides to rekindle Manchurian-Japanese relations and announces a series of cultural exchanges. The Japanese army, publicly praised and flattered by the Manchurian authorities, consents to forgive and manages to forget. We slip back into normality with no more fuss than the blinking of an eye. April brings us its radiant clarity. At school we start Japanese lessons again.

This morning I wake up late. My rickshaw boy runs breathlessly as fast as he can so that I am not late for school. He has sweat running down his back and great blue veins crawl over his arms, and I am so overcome with guilt that I ask him to slow down.

'Please don't worry, miss,' he replies haltingly, 'a good run in the morning is the secret of eternal life.'

In front of the Temple of the White Horse I catch sight of Min heading in the opposite direction on his bicycle. I am so amazed that I don't even think to wave a greeting . . . Our paths cross for a moment and then we are carried away from each other.

26

THE ORDER to leave is given. I have no time to say goodbye to Madame Violette and Masayo before our unit leaves the barracks and heads for the station. Whistles shriek on the platform and several companies of men push and jostle to get into the trains laden with tanks and munitions. We manage to climb up into a double-decker carriage.

The chill air of a hesitant, stuttering spring makes it impossible for me to sleep. I place my hand over my tunic pocket where I have put the last two letters I have received: they are still there. In Mother's, her fine, clear writing reassures me that she is well, at least temporarily alleviating my anxiety. Akiko has somehow got hold of my address and has written at length.

Before I left, this young woman came to bid me farewell, and I deliberately went to hide, hoping it would make her hate me. She was my younger sister's best friend and, having lost her brothers in the earthquake, she had become attached to me. Her family was related to the shogun Tokugawa,[1] and her modesty and elegance

1 Tokugawa's family produced fifteen shoguns, who reigned over Japan

had appealed to Mother, who secretly hoped we would be married. Encouraged by her own parents, the young girl already believed she was my intended. Once I had left the military academy and had taken up my post on the outskirts of Tokyo, she started to write to me at the barracks – I replied to one letter in four. When I was away she would come to visit my sister, and her smiling and bowing won over my landlady, who willingly opened my door for her. She would wash and iron my dirty laundry, and darn my socks. Like most well-brought-up women, Akiko never spoke to me of her feelings, but her discretion did not stop me from putting her squarely in her place: she would be a sister, and nothing more.

A few words from Miss Sunlight would certainly have given more pleasure than Akiko's endless missive. But I know that the geisha will never write to me. The life she has chosen is a whirlwind of parties, banquets, laughter and music. When will she have a quiet moment to think of me?

I passed through her life, but it was a one-way trip.

from the beginning of the seventeenth century to the end of the nineteenth century.

27

I HAVE been going past the Temple of the White Horse every morning for years, and Min has been taking the same route but in the other direction, although we have never seen each other. For the last week he has appeared just as the bells in the shrine have started to ring.

Before I leave the house I slip into Mother's bedroom and look at my reflection in her full-length oval mirror. My fringe looks childish now and, with the help of two grips set with tiny pearls that I have sighed and begged my way to borrowing from my sister, I hold it back and reveal my forehead.

As I reach the crossroads my heart beats so hard I can't catch my breath and I scour the streets anxiously for Min's bicycle. At last I see him toiling up a hill and, as he reaches the top, he stops and waves to me. At that moment, he is sharply silhouetted against the sky. The wind trips lightly through the branches, which are full of birds singing their joyful little musical score. Some young Taoist monks walk past in their grey tunics, eyes lowered. A street pedlar stokes his fire, and his fried rolls steam, giving off a delicious smell.

In class, instead of listening to the teacher, I review the image of Min on his bicycle a thousand times inside my head. I remember his eyes shining out from under his hat, the way he raises his arm in greeting with his books in his hand. My cheeks are burning, and I can't help smiling stupidly at the blackboard, where I think I can see him showing off as he weaves between the words and numbers.

28

A FTER THE earthquake I began to feel repulsed, but also fascinated, by death. These thoughts pursued me night and day: I would suddenly be overwhelmed with fear, I would have palpitations and I would cry for no reason.

The first time I touched a gun, I felt its strength in the chill of the steel. My first shooting lesson was outside, on an empty range. I was profoundly fearful, like a pilgrim preparing to touch the feet of a deity. With the first shot, my ears started to hum and, as the weapon kicked back, it struck me violently. That evening I went to bed with a sore shoulder, and a feeling of appeasement.

Every man has to die. Choosing oblivion is the only way of triumphing over this.

When I was sixteen I began to live again. At last I had stopped dreaming about tidal waves and ravaged forests. For me, the army was a giant arch capable of withstanding every kind of tempest. I was initiated into the delights of physical love in my very first year of cadet training, and I discovered the orgasmic pleasure of abandoning myself inside a woman. Then I learned to sacrifice pleasure to duty. The *Hagakure*[1] was like a beacon to me, guiding me through my adolescence towards maturity.

I prepared myself for death. Why should I marry? A samurai's wife kills herself when her husband dies. Why send another life hurtling into the abyss? I am fond of children, they are the continuation of a people, the hope of a nation, but I could never have my own. Children need to grow up with a father's guidance and protection, and to be spared from grief.

The appeal of a prostitute has the transient, furtive freshness of the morning dew. Prostitutes have no illusions and this makes them a soldier's natural soulmate. They respond with a blandness that is reassuring; as the daughters of poverty and misery, they have an abiding mistrust of happiness. Already damned, they dare not dream of eternity, and they cling to us like shipwrecked mariners clinging to flotsam. There is a religious purity in our embraces.

After our training we no longer had to hide our recreational activities. High-ranking officers openly kept geishas, and second lieutenants made do with more fleeting encounters.

I met Miss Sunlight in June 1931. We were in a teahouse celebrating our captain's promotion, and the screens slid silently backwards and forwards, revealing a steady stream of geishas. As one group arrived, the previous group was swallowed up in the shadows. Night had fallen along the Sumida, and boats with lanterns glided slowly downstream. I had been drinking and my

1 *Hagakure* by Jocho Yamamoto (1659–1719) is a code of conduct for samurais.

head was spinning. We were getting one of the officers drunk as he lost his hand at cards, and I kept roaring with laughter. I was just about to run outside to be sick when I caught sight of an apprentice geisha[1] wearing a blue kimono with wide, flowing sleeves with an iris design on them. She bowed deeply in greeting, moving slowly and with great nobility. Despite the white powder on her cheeks, the beauty spot that stood out against her chin made her look somehow melancholy.

She took a samisen from its case, picked up her ivory plectrum and tuned the instrument. She struck the strings abruptly and they reverberated loudly; it was like a clap of thunder in a summer sky. The wind blew, bending the trees and tearing open the inky clouds. The quiet clipping of the plectrum produced flashes of lightning that hurtled down the mountains. Waterfalls became torrents, rivers swelled and the sea, whipped up by the wind, hurled itself on the foaming shore. A husky voice began to sing of disappointed love, of abandonment and the underworld. I was seized by the misery that sometimes overwhelms a happy drunkard, and I was moved to tears by the desolate passion she described. Suddenly the music stopped, as abruptly as a vase breaking, and the voice fell silent.

All around me the officers were looking at each other, stunned and at a loss for words. After bidding us farewell, the apprentice geisha put away her samisen, gave a little bow and slipped away with a rustling of her kimono.

1 In Japan apprentice geishas wear wide sleeves. Once their status as geishas is confirmed, they wear narrow sleeves.

29

MOON PEARL keeps begging my parents to let me go with her to the new mayor's birthday celebrations. She is convinced that her husband will be going with his mistress, and is determined to catch him in flagrante.

Mother couldn't resist her tears. I find my sister's jealousy despicable, but I do want to get out and see people . . . and Min may be at the party.

'Ladies, good evening . . .'

The footmen at the bottom of the stairs greet us with effusive little bows. One of them goes ahead of us, inviting us to enter through a red lacquered gateway, and we walk across three successive courtyards. As Moon Pearl doesn't want her husband to see her, we have arrived after dark.

We are shown into a huge garden where about a hundred tables are dotted around under the trees and lit with good-luck lanterns to wish the mayor a long life. An orchestra in evening dress is battling desperately with its waltz tune against an opera troupe singing at the top of their lungs.

We wend our way discreetly towards a table sheltering

under an umbrella pine and settle there like two huntsmen waiting for their prey. To dispel the chill of early spring, our host has lit braziers and torches, and as soon as she sits down my sister complains that the flames are blinding her and she won't be able to recognise her unfaithful husband. I scour the area around us, looking for my brother-in-law, and I suddenly catch sight of Jing wearing a European suit and sitting alone at a table, away from the crowds. He is watching me.

I go and join him.

'Would you like some rice wine?' he asks.

'No, thank you, I can't stand it.'

On a sign from Jing, a waiter appears and dots a dozen dishes around the table. With a pair of chopsticks, Jing serves a few slices of translucent meat into a bowl for me.

'Taste it,' he says. 'It's the pad of a bear's paw.'

This meat, which is highly prized by the Manchurian aristocracy, slithers over my tongue. It doesn't taste of anything.

'Here,' he says, 'this is camel's foot marinated in wine for five years. And this is the fish they call black dragon, taken from the depths of the River Love.'

Instead of tasting the food, I ask him whether Min is here.

'No,' he says.

To hide my disappointment, I admit that I was dragged here by my sister and that I don't even know what our host, the new mayor, looks like. He points out a short, fat man of about fifty wearing a brocade tunic.

'How do you know him?'

'He's my father.'

'Your father!'

'You're surprised, aren't you?' says Jing with a cold

little laugh. 'Before the rebels attacked, he was a council member to the former mayor. One man's death is another man's making. My father would even manage to get himself promoted in hell!'

Embarrassed by his admission, I can't think how to move away.

'Look, that's one of my stepmothers,' says Jing, pointing rather obviously at a woman who is greeting the guests like a butterfly alighting on flowers to gather nectar. She is over-made-up and is wearing a richly embroidered tunic lined with fur, and a fan-shaped headdress scattered with pearls, coral, and muslin flowers – clearly a priceless antique.

'She was a whore before she became my father's concubine,' says Jing derisively. 'She sleeps with a Japanese colonel now. Do you know why she dresses herself up as an imperial lady-in-waiting? She has always claimed to be descended from a deposed family of the pure yellow banner[1] ... Now, this is my mother coming over. How can she accept that harlot under her roof?'

Following Jing's gaze, I can make out the silhouette of a middle-aged woman. Behind her I suddenly catch sight of my brother-in-law with his hair slicked back and wearing an ostentatiously elegant suit. I ask Jing whether he knows him.

A smile appears at the corners of his mouth.

'Is that your brother-in-law? The informer?'

'Why informer? My brother-in-law is a respected journalist.'

---

1 Manchurian hierarchy is classed in order according to different-coloured banners that represent the various clans. Pure yellow is the colour of the clan that counts the imperial family among its descendants.

Jing doesn't answer. He pours himself a large glass of wine and drinks it down in one. He is a friend of Min's, but he inspires a disturbing mixture of disgust and admiration in me. When I leave him, I feel so confused that I can no longer find my sister's table.

30

MY FRIENDS persuaded themselves that I had fallen for the apprentice geisha and they invited her to our banquets as often as possible. I flushed every time she appeared. The winks and stifled laughs that my brother officers exchanged irritated me, even though they also gave me an obscure feeling of pride and happiness.

Sunlight was shy, and she always left quickly after she had sung, but as time went by she agreed to serve us food and to have a drink. She had tiny hands and her fingernails were like antique pearls. When she brought her glass up to her lips, the sleeve of her kimono slipped down her arm, revealing a dazzlingly white wrist. Would it be like gazing on a snowfield to see her naked?

My pay at the time only just allowed for me to arrange the occasional dinner and I was in no position to keep a geisha. Time went by and my ardour cooled; I needed more accessible women to brighten the stark austerity of military life.

The political landscape that year was like a leaden sky: we dreamed that the storm would break, letting the sun shine through once more. As soldiers, we could neither take a step back nor shy away from the situation, and a number of lieutenants[1] chose martyrdom. There were more and more assassinations, and the young assassins would then hand themselves over to the authorities to prove their loyalty. But neither their own terror nor these voluntary deaths could do anything to jolt our ministers out of their inertia. They were so afraid of a return to the Kamakura era[2] that their only thought was to keep the military as far from power as possible.

We were coming close to the moment of ultimate sacrifice: in order to conquer the world we had to cross a bridge made of our own flesh and blood. Seppuku[3] became fashionable again, a noble form of suicide that requires a long period of mental preparation, and this turned my thoughts away from the apprentice geisha.

One spring day I received a mysterious letter written in a beautiful calligraphy that betrayed its writer's rigorous education. A woman I did not know asked me to meet her in a tea-house by the Bridge of Willows. Intrigued, I went to the rendezvous. Night was closing in, I could hear music and laughter in the distance, but the rustling of silk just the other side of the door suggested geishas were passing behind it. Then the screens drew apart and a woman of about forty greeted me with a bow. She wore a kimono in greyish-pink silk

1 On 15th May 1932 nine officers managed to get into Prime Minister Inukai's residence. They assassinated him before handing themselves over to the police.

2 The Kamakura era: 1192–1333. While the Emperor continued to preside over a symbolic court in Kyoto, the shogun in Kamakura actually wielded power over the entire country.

3 A form of suicide accessible only to samurais (and, therefore, only to men). It follows a precise ritual: death is achieved by disembowelment with a small sabre.

with glimpses at the neck of a second, olive-green kimono. A hand-painted cherry tree in blossom scattered its petals over her kimono right to the very ends of her sleeves.

She introduced herself as Sunlight's mother and welcomed me. I had heard that she herself was a former geisha and that she owned a large tea-house. She told me that she had known my father; I knew that he had been very much in love with a geisha, and asked whether it was she.

She stared at me intently for a moment, then lowered her eyes.

'You have met my daughter,' she said. 'Have you enjoyed the evenings you have spent in her company?'

I told her that I very much admired her talents as a musician.

'My daughter is seventeen. She should have moved on and been confirmed as a geisha last year. As you probably know, in this profession an apprentice geisha cannot be given an artist's status until she has undergone the *mizu-age* ceremony. My own experience was worse than a nightmare and I have decided to spare my daughter from a similar calamity. I have asked her to choose her man, and she has chosen you. I have taken the liberty of finding out about you, and you have been spoken of most highly. You are on the threshold of a great military career, but you are young and you would never be able to pay the sum required for this ceremony. That does not matter; I have chosen for my daughter to be happy and I offer her body to you. If you accept this humble request, I shall be eternally grateful to you.'

I was completely astonished by what she had said, and I

did not say a word. She came towards me on her knees and bowed low.

'I beg you to consider it,' she said. 'Do not trouble yourself with the financial details, I shall take care of that. Consider it, please . . .'

She stood up and disappeared behind the screens. I found the room oppressively dark. According to tradition, an apprentice geisha should be deflowered by a rich stranger. This initiation is expensive, but it is the crowning status symbol for a man of the world. No apprentice geisha has ever chosen the man who should ravish her, and I had just been asked to transgress this custom scandalously.

I was tormented with doubt and could not give my answer straight away.

31

I DIDN'T see Min yesterday on my way to school and I keep asking myself whether he is ill or whether he doesn't want to see me any more. Is he already engaged, like many students of his age? Why should he show any interest in a schoolgirl?

He isn't at the crossroads this morning, either. Feeling sad and indignant, I am just deciding I will have to forget him when a series of ringing sounds attracts my attention: I look up and see Min pedalling towards me.

'What are you doing this afternoon?' he cries.

'I'm playing go on the Square of a Thousand Winds,' I can't help myself answering.

'You can do that another day. I'm inviting you out to lunch,' he says and, without giving me time to decline his invitation, he adds, 'I'll wait for you when you come out of school.'

Before riding past us he throws me a banknote.

'It's for your rickshaw boy,' he says, 'it'll keep him quiet.'

At noon I come out of school after everyone else and, head lowered, I make my way along the wall. Min is not at the door. I heave a sigh of relief and get into a rickshaw, but then he looms in front of me like a ghost.

He abandons his bicycle and slips onto the seat beside me before I even have time to cry out in surprise. He puts one arm around my shoulders and with the other hand he lowers the blind on the rickshaw so that we are hidden down to our knees. Then he tells the boy to take us to the Hill of Seven Ruins.

The rickshaw trundles through the narrow streets. Inside, sheltered from the stares of passers-by under the white tenting yellowed by the sun, Min's breathing becomes heavier. He brushes my neck lightly with his fingers then buries them in my hair, massaging the back of my neck. I hold my breath, rigid with terror and with an unfamiliar feeling of delight. Beneath the bottom of the blind I can see the rickshaw boy's legs swinging regularly. Dogs, children and pedestrians skim by on the pavements to either side . . . I would like this monotonous landscape to go on for ever.

On Min's orders, the rickshaw boy stops outside a restaurant. Min sits himself down as if he were in his own home and orders some noodles. The tiny room is soon filled with the smell of cooking, which blends with the scent of the first spring flowers. The manager serves us and goes back to snooze behind his counter as the midday sun streams in through the open door. I concentrate silently on my food while Min holds forth on the class struggle. When he interrupts himself to say he has never seen a girl eat as voraciously as me, I don't rise to his teasing – I find the whole situation exasperating! This young man is obviously accustomed to this sort of tête-à-tête, but I have no idea how a girl in my position should behave. Min saves me from my own confusions by suggesting we go for a walk on the Hill of Seven Ruins.

We start our climb along a shady path where all around us yellow dandelions and purple campanula are in flower. The new grass has grown in dense clumps round the charred granite blocks, the vestiges of a palace that was consumed in flames. Min asks me to sit down on a lotus flower carved in marble, and he stands back to look at me. I find the silence uncomfortable, and sit with my head lowered, bending a buttercup stem with the tip of my shoe.

I don't know what to do. In the novels at school – *Mandarin Ducks* and *Wild Butterflies* – a description of a young man and a young woman in a garden would constitute the most awkward scene in a love story: they have so much to say to each other, but a sense of propriety forbids them from betraying their emotions. By comparing the two of us to characters in the sort of books you buy at a train station, I eventually think we are both ridiculous. What does Min expect of me? And what do I expect of him?

I don't feel anything to compare with the thrill of our first meeting, or with the palpitations I feel every morning as I travel to school and Min simply passes by me. Is our story already coming to an end, and does love exist only in the solitude of my imagination?

Min suddenly puts his hand on my shoulder, making me quiver. I am just about to break free from him when he starts to stroke my face with the tips of his fingers, my eyebrows, eyelids, forehead, chin. Each little move he makes sends shivers through me. My cheeks are burning and I feel ashamed, I am afraid we will be seen through the foliage . . . but I don't have the strength to resist.

He draws my head to his; his face approaches one centimetre at a time. I can make out the freckles on his cheeks, the beginnings of a moustache, the misgiving in his eyes. I am too proud to let my fears show and so, instead of fighting, I fall straight into his arms. His lips brush gently onto mine. They are dry but his tongue is moist, and I am amazed when I feel it probe into my mouth. A torrent flows over me.

I have to cry, but the tears won't come. I scratch his back and he groans. With eyes closed, cheeks flaming and blue rings under his eyes, Min kisses me with the desperate ardour of a collector who has made a rare discovery.

Above the tops of the trees, the town melts away in a light mist. My silence doesn't discourage him: he takes me to the monastery at the top of the hill and orders some tea from a young monk. After filling my cup, he snaps open some watermelon seeds and looks out over the view, whistling. Avoiding his eyes, and the eyes of the monks who are staring at me, I drain my cup of tea, get up, smooth my crumpled skirt and go back down the steps four at a time.

The sun is sinking, a mask of red lacquer. Beyond the city walls, the melting snow reveals the scorched earth beneath. The villages blend into the parcels of black soil, and the trees flatten out and disappear into the surrounding folds created by the cloak of twilight.

That night I dream that Cousin Lu bursts into my room, comes over to me, takes my hand and presses it to his chest. I am disgusted and I try to shake him off, but his fingers are insistent and I can feel their heat. A strange languorous feeling washes over me.

Horrified, I wake to find I am bathed in sweat.

32

A T THE beginning of that autumn I received a letter from a woman asking me to meet her in a park. I was sure she had been sent for my answer on the subject of the apprentice geisha, and I went to the assigned place at ten o'clock in the morning, having made up my mind to say no.

A woman sat under a flaming maple on a stone bench dotted with rust-coloured lichen. Her hair was knotted in a simple chignon and she was wearing an indigo-blue cotton kimono held at the waist with an orange belt.

I could not believe my eyes: it was Sunlight but, without make-up, her pale lips scarcely pink, she looked like a child of ten. She stood up and bowed in greeting.

'Thank you for coming,' she said.

We sat perched at either end of the bench. She had her back half-turned to me and she remained completely silent.

I could not find the words I had prepared.

After a long while, I asked whether she would like to walk in the park. She walked behind me, taking tiny steps. All the maples were ablaze and the ginkgoes were a bright yellow; the autumn wind wafted their fiery leaves over us. We crossed a wooden bridge, went round a pool of emerald-green water bordered with chrysanthemums, and came to a stop in an open pavilion from which we could gaze out at the cloudless sky and decorative rocks crawling with ivy. The only sounds were the rustling of her kimono and the birdsong. Our mutual silence was complicit. I could not break it.

As we left the park, she bowed deeply and walked away.

33

O N THE Square of a Thousand Winds I am playing
against Wu, the antique dealer, having agreed to
give him eight handicap points. When he is beaten, he
slinks away with a sigh.

Just one game of go is enough to exhaust most players.
They need to eat and sleep in order to return to their
normal state, but I react differently: my mind is whirring
from the very beginning of the game, and the effort of
concentration stimulates a paroxysm of excitement in me.
For hours after the game is over I don't know how to let
out the force that's accumulated within me, and I search
in vain for some form of release.

Today, like every other day, I head for home, taking
great powerful strides. The most extraordinary daydreams
come to me: I feel as if I no longer belong to the world of
mortals; I see myself joining the ranks of the gods.

A man calls out to me and I look up and see Jing
crossing the road on a bicycle. There's a birdcage covered
in a blue cloth behind him on his bicycle rack. He brakes
alongside me.

'What are you doing here with that cage?'

He tears off the cloth and proudly shows off two robins.

'These birds love going out for a ride. Usually people swing the cage along as they go for their morning walk. But I could die of boredom walking like an old man, so this is my latest invention.'

I laugh, and he asks whether I would like him to take me home. Darkness has fallen and I can no longer make out the faces of the passers-by: I can climb onto his bicycle with no fear of being recognised. I'm holding the cage with my left arm and I put my right arm round Jing's waist. He sets off and I have to cling to his waistcoat to keep my balance. My fingers slip on the silk and fur, holding firm on a level with his stomach. Under the fur-lined waistcoat he is wearing a cotton tunic. The warmth of his skin burns my hand through the weave of the fabric. With each movement of his legs, the muscles contract and relax beneath my fingers. Disconcerted, I remove my arm, but Jing then leans into a corner, forcing me to hold him all the more tightly.

I ask him to stop beside the back door. The street has high walls on both sides and is poorly lit by one feeble street lamp. Jing's cheeks are burning red, he is breathing noisily and fumbling for his handkerchief.

I press mine to his forehead. He thanks me and wipes his face, which is dripping with sweat. Embarrassed by my watching him, he turns towards the wall and unbuttons his tunic to run the handkerchief over his chest. I ask whether he has any news of Min.

'I'm seeing him tomorrow at the university . . .'

I hand the cage to him and he takes it firmly in his arms.

'Your hankie smells nice,' he says, almost in a whisper.

A loud clatter makes us both start: the bicycle was not properly balanced against the tree and it has fallen over. Jing bends over, picks it up and flees like a hunted hare.

34

THE TRAIN comes to a sharp halt. The jolt tears me from my sleep and I hear the order to start marching. As I get out of the carriage, dawn clasps me in its icy fingers. Under a sky tinged with the tiniest hint of mauve, the scorched earth lies uninterrupted as far as the eye can see: not one crop, not a single tree.

The train leaves and we envy our comrades who are travelling on into the inner territories. Our detachment has responsibility for the security of a small town in southern Manchuria, with the curious name of A Thousand Winds.

Huddling my neck right down inside the collar of my uniform, I continue to doze and let the rhythm of the marching carry me along. In just a few months I have learned to sleep and walk at the same time. The regular swinging of my legs warms me and the rocking motion soothes me.

The 'wedding night' took place in a pavilion in the middle of the park where Sunlight had already asked me to meet her. After dinner a young servant girl took me to a bedroom where a futon had been unfolded. She helped me to undress and to put on a *yukata*. I lay down on my back with my arms crossed and tried to gather my thoughts.

I did not know the time, but it must have been late. The silence was oppressive; it was hot. I got up and pulled aside the screens that led out onto the veranda.

The moon was ringed with opaque clouds, and the croaking toads and sighing crickets seemed to be answering each other's calls in the darkness. I closed the doors and went back to the bed. My feeling of intoxication melted away as I became increasingly impatient. I had never come across virginity, so how would I know what to do?

An almost imperceptible sound made me look up. Sunlight was standing in the doorway, draped in a white kimono. She bowed slightly. Her face was painted in a regal mask, which made her seem all the more inaccessible. She crossed the room silently like a ghost and shut herself in the next room.

She came back out without her ceremonial kimono, but wrapped in a crimson *yukata*. Her jet-black hair stood out against the fiery silk. She was just a little girl.

She sat for a long time with her hands on her knees, staring into space, then suddenly broke the silence: 'Take me in your arms, please.'

I held her awkwardly, pressing my cheek against hers. Her perfume wafted from the neckline of her *yukata*, making my heart pound.

She lay with her arms by her sides as if she were dead. When I parted her legs she nervously held me to her with all her might. I had to force open her tightly clamped thighs and found that she was icy-cold between her legs. I was dripping with sweat and my sweat mingled with hers, carving dark furrows through her white make-up. Her soaked hair snaked across her cheeks, sometimes creeping into my mouth. She was like a strangled animal, unable to let out even the slightest sound. I wanted to kiss her, but I found the bright-red lipstick repulsive. I stroked her body, enveloped as it was in the *yukata*. It felt clammy and feverish, and her flesh puckered into goose pimples wherever my fingers touched. In the depths of her pupils I suddenly saw the same terrible fear I had seen in the eyes of condemned men before their execution.

I felt crushed and overwhelmingly discouraged. I let myself fall away from her body and went down on my knees.

'What is it?' she asked in a wavering voice.

'I'm so sorry.'

She burst into tears. 'Oh, please.'

Her despair was indescribably distressing for me too. I thought I knew about women but, at twenty, I did not yet know that beyond the realms of pleasure, men enter a twilight world where dignity is lost and where devastated souls stumble through the darkness masked like performers in the theatre of Noh. I decided to cover her face with the sheet in which we were both lying and to lift up the bottom of her *yukata*. In the lamplight her legs looked deathly pale. The long cleft between her legs had sleek fur like an otter. I tried to imagine she was just a prostitute picked up in the street. I could not think of her as just a cavity to be filled by a triumphant phallus seeking its glorious release.

I masturbated, but my member did not respond. Seeing how still the young girl was, I thought suddenly that she had suffocated and was lying there dead.

I lifted the sheet: Sunlight was crying.

To save face, I cut my arm with a dagger and let my blood flow onto the strip of white cloth that was meant to be coloured by her virginal blood. A little before dawn, I helped her repowder her face. She rolled up the bloodied strip, put it up her sleeve and left.

35

HUONG COMES home with me after lessons today. We have supper with my parents and then shut ourselves in my room to play a game of chess.

'I'm going to be married,' she announces, advancing her knight.

'Now, that's good news,' I say, convinced she is joking. 'Who's the lucky man? Do I know him?'

She doesn't answer and I look up to see her holding a pawn between her fingers, resting her cheek on her left hand. The lamplight picks out two lines of tears running down her nose. Horrified, I beg her to talk, but she breaks down and cries.

I watch her with a tight sensation round my heart: since I met Min and Jing, Huong has become less important to me. The parties don't seem so much fun any more and I refuse all her invitations. When she walks home with me after school, I hardly listen to her chattering – my mind is on other things.

'I'm engaged.'

'Who to?'

She stares at me for a long time. 'The younger son of the mayor of our town.'

I roar with laughter.

'Where on earth did he spring from? You've never told me about him. Why were you hiding him? You must have played green plums and bamboo horses together when you were children, and then bumped into him one day in town. Where is he studying? Is he good-looking? I hope you're going to live here. Look, I can't see why you're crying. Is there some problem?'

'I've never met him. My father and stepmother decided for me. I have to go back to the country at the end of July.'

'Don't tell me they're forcing you to marry a stranger!'

Huong cries all the more desperately.

'They can't be,' I say indignantly. 'Surely you're not going to accept this nonsense? Times have changed. Nowadays girls don't belong body and soul to their parents.'

'My father's written to me . . . If I refuse, he'll stop . . . he'll stop supporting me . . .'

'The bastard! You're not some product, or something that can be bartered! You've just escaped from your stepmother's clutches. You're not going to let yourself fall into the hands of a mother-in-law, some rural harridan who smokes a pipe and is drugged on opium, and envies you because you're young and well educated. She'll humiliate you and belittle you until you're like her – frustrated, sulky and nasty. You'll have a great fat father-in-law who spends his evenings with prostitutes and comes home blind-drunk and shouts at your husband. Your husband will get bored with you; you'll live in a huge house surrounded by women: servants, cooks, your father-in-law's concubines, your husband's concubines, sisters-in-law, the mothers and sisters of your sisters-in-law, and they'll all be scheming to attract the men's attention and to stab you in the back. You'll be given children: if you have a son you'll be respected, but if you have a daughter they'll treat you like their dogs or their pigs. Then one day they'll renounce you in a letter and you'll bring nothing but shame on your family . . .'

'Stop it, please . . .' cries Huong, stifled by her tears.

Knowing that I have made her suffer, I go to fetch a damp towel. I make her clean up her face and drink a cup of tea.

She calms down a little.

'I know it's difficult to disobey your father. In the past, disobedience was a crime, but nowadays it's the only way of ensuring your happiness. If your father stops supporting you, my parents will help you. We'll go to university together. Come on.'

Dragging Huong by the hand, I go over to the little red lacquered cupboard where I keep my treasures, and remove the padlock. Among the books, the scrolls of calligraphy and the phials of ink in their wooden case, I find my embroidered silk purse. I open it under the lamp and show Huong my jewels.

'We'll sell them. They'll pay for our studies.'

Her tears well up again immediately.

'My mother left me hers. My father took them from me to give to his new wife.'

'Stop snivelling. If you have a choice between money and freedom, you mustn't hesitate for a moment. Now, dry your tears. Everything that is mine is yours. Stop torturing yourself.'

It is well into the night, and Huong has slipped into

96

restless sleep beside me. I listen to the wind and the cats running along the rooftops.

The image of my sister Moon Pearl comes into my mind: her legs are svelte, fine as bamboo stalks. She is proudly showing me the present my brother-in-law gave her for their reconciliation, a pair of milky-white satin shoes embroidered with tiny butterflies. Her naked foot inside this dazzling shoe is as beautiful as her hand, gloved in silk and bearing a pink coral ring. Then the happiness falls from her face. She looks pale, her hair is unkempt, she has dark rings under her eyes and lines on her forehead. Her eyes are lifeless, and she stares vacantly into the distance. She is counting the minutes and praying that her husband will be home before midnight. There is something terrible about this body already withering with old age and ugliness. To me, Moon Pearl is not a woman but a flower that is slowly wilting.

My mother is not a woman, either: she belongs to the race of the crucified. I see her copying out Father's manuscript and researching information for him. Her eyesight is failing, her back hurts, she is wearing herself out for something that will never bear her name. When Father is maligned and persecuted by his jealous colleagues, she consoles him and defends him. Three years ago, when he had a child with a young student, she hid her pain, and when the girl came to our door one morning with the baby in her arms, Mother gave her everything she had and then sent her away. She bought peace in our household at the expense of her own soul. She never cried once.

But who really deserves to be called a woman?

36

I WENT back to the prostitutes: I found them reassuring and I was sure they would give me an erection, but I was so haunted by the image of Sunlight that my moment of ecstasy was shot through with pain. The geisha now had a banker as her protector, and she was beginning to make a reputation for herself. It was not long before she moved only in the most elevated circles and I lost track of her.

I saw her again one misty evening two years later, climbing into a rickshaw on the other side of the road. She was wearing a heavy, rounded headdress and a sumptuous coat. She saw me, pretended not to notice and glided off into the darkness like a goddess returning to the heavens.

When I returned from my posting in Manchuria, I went to her house and her mother invited me in. I waited in a silent room, sipping *sake* for what seemed like a long time. Late into the night she came home from an official reception, wearing a black kimono which had golden waves embroidered along the hem over a hand-painted grey sea. Her hair was wet because of the thin, icy rain, and she wiped her handkerchief over it. I had not seen her for years: the slight hollowness of her cheeks accentuated the hard look in her eye. She seemed exhausted, spent. As I studied her face – which had become the face of a woman – I felt I had been betrayed.

She sat down opposite me with her eyes lowered and her hands on her knees, and her shyness reminded me of our walk in the park. We sat in silence for a long time: a great river lay between us and neither of us had the strength to cross it.

'I'm leaving for Manchuria.'

She was unmoved, she did not even blink.

'I shall never forget you,' she said.

Those words were enough; I bowed deeply and got to my feet. She stayed there motionless. There was not a tear or even the slightest sigh to mark this bitter, liberating farewell.

37

As I come out of school I see Min leaning up against a tree. I catch his eye and then lower my head and continue on my way.

'Do you mind if I walk with you for a while?' he says, running after me.

I don't say anything and he shamelessly tags along and chatters away to me. In fact I don't mind having him beside me; he is head and shoulders taller than me and I find the warm flow of his words soothing. He tells me about what he is reading, what he has been hunting and about his dreams of revolution. He asks whether I would like to go fishing on Sunday, whether I would like him to teach me how to know when fish are in love.

We go past the street where Jing lives.

'Come,' he says, pulling my arm, 'I've got a key.'

Once we are inside, he turns to me and looks me up and down. His nerve is disarming and I huddle against the door, powerless.

He starts stroking my face and neck, his fingers brushing my shoulders. I succumb to a strange languorous feeling that sweeps over me. Min's face is flushed and his eyes half-closed as he breathes in the smell of my skin. As his lips touch me they leave a trail of fever in their wake. When they reach my chin, I involuntarily open my mouth and Min's tongue darts in. As his hand moves down to my breast, his touch becomes almost unbearable, the warmth of his embrace suffocating. I tell him to open the top of my dress. He seems amazed, but obeys me. His fingers fumble hopelessly with the braided buttons and I almost tear them open.

Min's face twists into a grimace of admiration. He kneels down and buries his head between my breasts, rubbing his soft adolescent beard against them. His forehead feels white-hot, and makes me writhe. I clench my fists.

A scraping sound in the keyhole makes us both start, and I quickly push Min away. I have only just buttoned my dress when the door opens and Jing comes in, carrying his birdcage in his hand. The smile leaves his face when he sees us. He eyes me coldly and grunts a greeting to Min. I pick up my bag, barge past Jing and run off down the road.

Never before have I felt gripped by such sadness. The crows caw and wheel past each other across the sky where violet and orange gradually blend with the black of the clouds. The air is filled with the smell of flowers. With the arrival of the month of May, the poplar flowers fall to the ground like brown worms. As a child I used to throw them down my sister's open collar and she would scream in terror.

Min kneaded my breasts so hard they are hurting. I stop under a tree to tidy my hair and to smooth out my dress with a bit of saliva in the palm of my hand. I look at myself in a little mirror: my mouth looks slightly swollen as if I have just woken from a long sleep. My cheeks are bright red, betraying my secret, forbidden dreams, and my forehead is glowing, I think that I can trace Min's kisses on it, visible only to me.

38

WE HAVE polished our weapons and sorted out our creased uniforms before setting off again. Soon an ancient city looms on the horizon, surrounded by ramparts and with poplar trees lining the moat. Along the route there are Chinese people waving our rising-sun flags. Once we have passed through the main gate, the wealth of the town of A Thousand Winds is spread out before us: an endless expanse of tiled roofs, wide streets seething with traders and salesmen, the deafening sound of the traffic and appetising smells from the restaurants. A colonel from the garrison comes towards us, flanked by officers and followed by the town's mayor, a podgy Manchurian with a moustache and his attendant representatives of the local bourgeoisie.

We cannot believe our eyes: on the pavement there are about thirty young prostitutes draped in kimonos, laughing, blushing, jostling each other and beckoning us. The shyest among them hide behind their hands as they pass comments about our faces and figures. The bolder ones string together a few words of Japanese for us: 'So good-looking!', 'Come and see me at the Golden Lotus',

'I love you'. Forgetting how tired we are from marching, we look up proudly and take lungfuls of air to puff out our chests.

The barracks are over to the west of town, with barricades and machine guns on the gates, and barbed wire along the tops of the walls. The reserve detachment has lined up in four square formations on the parade ground to greet us.

After the welcoming parade comes the hot meal: in the canteen we hardly wait for the speeches to end before throwing ourselves on the seaweed soup with spicy beef; we fight over the plump carp, the haunches of venison and the pheasant breasts. We gulp down rice balls, marinated vegetables, *dofus* and raw fish beautifully laid out on dishes.

With my belly distended like a balloon and still ruminating on the vanished flavours, I drag myelf to my room and collapse on the bed.

39

MIN PUTS on a mysterious expression and boasts that he has copies of books that have been banned by the government: he is trying to get me to go over to Jing's house. Just thinking about the place makes me feel giddy, but I really have to make up my mind. There will be no going back. I am no longer – nor do I still want to be – just a little schoolgirl, happy to sit and dream. Now I must do something, take a leap into the unknown. When the irreversible starts to happen, then, in that moment, I will know at last who I am and why I am alive.

In the library Min exhumes his 'dangerous' volumes from their hiding places under piles of old books. I turn the pages, devouring the words with my eyes. Min takes the opportunity to come behind me and wrap his arms round me. His hands roam under my dress and close over my breasts.

He undresses me as if he were peeling a piece of fruit. Still in my knickers and with my arms crossed over my breasts, I tell him to put my skirt on a hanger without creasing it. Then he undresses, throwing his clothes to the four corners of the room. With his underpants still on, he throws himself at me and rubs his chest against mine.

I close my eyes and try to struggle against the weight of his body as Min forcibly drags me to the middle of the room and lies me down on a desk. He slowly parts my legs and I put my hands out to hide myself, but he catches hold of my arms. I twist and struggle, moaning. Trying to calm me, he kisses the end of my nipple and sucks it. I cry out in pain. He draws himself up to his full height, looming above me like a demon, as if his head were touching the ceiling. His tormented face is etched against the square of blue sky framed by the window. He stands there, his stomach between my thighs, and then suddenly moves forward.

According to legend, one form of torture that the devils in hell particularly favour is slicing the damned in half: in the popular imagination this image probably owes its origins to the first encounter between a man and a woman.

'Did it hurt?'

I bite my lower lip and refuse to say anything.

Min looks at me for a moment, then gets dressed and wipes my face with a handkerchief. He gazes into my eyes and says, 'I must marry you.'

'Take me over to the bed.'

Min closes the doors, draws the curtains and lets down the mosquito netting round the bed. We wrap ourselves in a silk cover lined with cotton. I lie there in the half-light, paralysed by the smell of rotting wood.

'It always feels a bit strange the first time,' he says comfortingly.

'You must be pretty experienced to say that!'

He doesn't say anything, but lets his hands wander

over my neck, shoulders, arms and stomach. Outside the cicadas are beginning to sing. Min is on top of me again; it hurts, but this time the surgery is more bearable. I am shaking and short of breath, my head is spinning and everything is confused. I think I see Jing, and then Cousin Lu.

Suddenly Min stares at me with a cruel but anxious glint in his eye. He lets out a series of involuntary, hoarse groans. After struggling against some invisible force, he falls down on top of me, inert.

He goes straight to sleep with his tired arms around my waist and his head nestling in the crook of my neck. Every time I move, he instinctively strokes me and draws me closer to him. I have to go back to school, but I don't want to get up. Tomorrow I will use lies to help me; but for now my thoughts are roaming like the clouds that scud across the sky above our town to run aground behind the mountains, to the north of the Manchurian plain. I have heard that virgins lose a lot of blood, but I haven't bled at all. The gods have spared me this violence that terrifies so many women. I don't feel guilty, but pleased: life has never seemed so simple or so clear.

At the end of the afternoon we go back to the outside world. Night is already falling, but the day still hangs in the air, a ship seeking its harbour. I remember my piano lesson and think up an excuse that will convince my mother. I walk slowly. Something that has always been buried in the depths of me has been exhumed, like a sheet taken out of a trunk and aired in the sunlight. My virginity is nothing but a wound; my body has been cleaved apart, it is open and the breeze blows through me.

Min shakes me out of my reverie. 'When we've seen off the Japanese, I'll marry you.'

'I don't want to get married. Go and take care of the revolution.'

He stops and looks at me with a hurt expression and a trembling lip. He is so good-looking!

'My family is descended from the yellow banner. Our land extends from the ramparts of the town all the way to the steppes of Mongolia. My father is dead and I want to dedicate my inheritance to my country's freedom. I will be poor and I will live dangerously. As you have given me the most precious thing you have, unless you despise me, you shall be my wife.'

I start to laugh.

In the rickshaw I raise one arm to wave goodbye. Min stands on the pavement and his silhouette gradually dissolves into a dark shape and then a hazy blur against the darkness of the town.

40

As a child my dreams were fuelled by the mystery of the Middle Empire. I liked drawing Mandarin pavilions, Tatar strongholds and imperial warriors. Later I devoured its classical literature.

Until yesterday the only part of China that I knew was Ha Rebin, the huge metropolis on the banks of the River Love, and that modern, cosmopolitan place now serves as my yardstick: I keep comparing the town of A Thousand Winds to it. This small city may well be a part of independent Manchuria, but it is instantly recognisable as a little chunk of the eternal Chinese nation.

There are fewer cars here than in Ha Rebin, and there are no trams. Hundreds of rickshaw boys work in shifts day and night, and bicycles are the prized possessions of students from wealthy families.

Unlike the population of Ha Rebin – a coarse-looking people descended from the exiled and the condemned – the natives here have delicate features. Their ancestors are said to have been the illegitimate offspring of princes, the blood flowing in their veins is a subtle blend of Manchurian, Mongolian and Chinese. Their faces, with their regular features, seem to recall those of centuries long past. The men are tall, with darker skin and eyes that are slit right to the temple. The women have inherited their fairer skin, high cheekbones, almond eyes and tiny mouths from the ladies of the court.

The very day after we arrive some of the reserve officers take us off round the brothels just outside the garrison. I am convinced that prostitution was invented for the military and that the first prostitute in history was a woman who fell in love with a soldier.

Here, just as in Japan, the girls try to separate us from our savings with their charming smiles. The Chinese girls stammer just enough rudimentary Japanese to agree a price. Some of the brothels are run by our army, and these employ Japanese and Korean girls, but the prices are prohibitive. Unable to afford a compatriot, I take advice from those who know their way around, and they take me to a modest-looking establishment called the Jade Flute. In the middle of the courtyard a tree stretches up towards the sky, and on the floor above I catch glimpses of uniforms, tumbling hair and silky dresses.

The manageress, a woman with a thick Shan Dong accent, asks the girls to parade past us. I choose Orchid, who has slanting eyes like a she-wolf and a tiny, dark mouth like a crushed blueberry. Holding her cigarette between the tips of her fingers, with a fox tail slung over her shoulder and her bare feet in stiletto shoes, she swings her hips as she climbs the stairs ahead of me.

Almost before we have touched, she tells me seriously that she is a pure Manchurian and should not be taken for a Chinese girl. Unlike Japanese prostitutes – who hold themselves back and act out their pleasure – Orchid, this daughter of the banner, succumbs and cries out. It is rare to see a prostitute having an orgasm, but there is a disarming naivety and willingness in the way she abandons herself. When I leave this girl with her powerful, well-muscled buttocks, she leans against the doorpost, waving her green handkerchief at me.

41

A T SCHOOL the next day there is a glint of pride in my eye. Yesterday's pain is still there, inside my body, burning me and eating me up – it gives me dignity. I still wear my blue dress just like the others, but I know that I am different now.

After lessons, I make a detour to go and see my sister. She is sitting by the window knitting, and I lie down opposite her on a willow couch.

Her sister-in-law has just announced that she is pregnant, and Moon Pearl bemoans the fact that her belly is still empty. I try to take her mind off this obsession by asking her, 'How do you know if you're in love?'

She wipes her tears and bursts out laughing.

'Well, well, have you found a boy you like? Why are you asking?'

'If you're not going to answer,' I say, pretending to be put out, 'I'll leave.'

'Are you angry? Don't you want some cake – it's honey and acacia-flower?' and she rings for the servant and carries on with her knitting before asking, 'What do you want to know?'

I hide my head behind a cushion. 'How do you know if you're in love? What does it feel like?'

'Well, first of all, you completely forget the world around you. Your friends and family just become invisible. All you can do is think about him day and night. When you see him, it's as if he's filled your eyes with light; and when you don't see him, the thought of him eats away at your heart. You wonder where he is and what he's doing every minute of the day. You invent his whole life, you live it for him: your eyes see for him, your ears hear for him . . .'

Moon Pearl takes a sip of tea before going on, 'In this first stage you don't know what the other is thinking or feeling. It's the most poignant part. Then you open your hearts to each other and you have a brief moment of incredible happiness . . .' She drops what she is doing and gazes out of the window.

'After the sunshine comes the storm,' she goes on. 'Suddenly you're thrown into darkness, you have to feel your way and crawl along carefully as you get older. You'll see, Little Sister, when you love and are loved by someone, you'll know the pain of living on a white-hot grill. You won't be sure of anything any more.'

My sister's lips are sore and cracked like arid soil. A look of hatred glowers in her eyes as she struggles to find someone to blame for her unhappiness. But then she says, 'You will have a happier fate. You are stronger than I am, you'll find a way of confronting the pain and appeasing the anger of the gods who are jealous of our love.'

'Well, why do people get married then?'

'Marriage?' she asks with a mocking laugh. 'It's cold and bland, it's a ceremony that we act out for our parents' sake. I've been reduced to my own shadow. The family I have built around me weighs me down, and some days I wish I was just a piece of furniture with no feelings and nothing to think about; then I'd know how to wait for him, how best to serve him, to make his home and honour his ancestors.'

Moon Pearl gets to her feet, picks a cluster of wisteria flowers and crushes them between her trembling fingers. 'I'm going to tell you the truth: I loved my husband. I gave him everything. I was like a silkworm, spewing the best of me from my insides, and now I'm just a barren husk. I know what I have to do now: I'll give him my life. Let him live and I'll die!'

I suddenly feel very uncomfortable and I give her the first excuse I can think of to get away. Out on the street I start to run; I need to breathe in this life, the trees, the warmth of my town. I will be able to control my own fate and I will know how to be happy. Happiness is something you lay siege to, it is a battle like a game of go. I will take hold of all the pain and snuff it out.

42

THE HEAT is making it difficult for us to get on with our training. Outside the walls of the town, the black of the open country is slowly turning into a sheet of burning-hot metal. Under the watchful eyes of the officers, the soldiers have to march, to run, to jump, to crawl, to shoot, and to bury their bayonets in the innards of straw dummies a thousand times. Those that pass out get a bucket of water poured over them and a couple of slaps in the face, but the Chinese recruits are punished more severely. It is as if our men are pieces of iron that need beating out to make useful weapons.

On the very first day my face caught the sun and my lips peeled. I have gone hoarse from shouting orders and my throat is burning; when I swallow a mouthful of rice it feels like grains of sand. The temperatures plummet at night, but our bodies still burn with the day's sun. The cold and the heat are too much for me and I toss and turn on my bed, unable to sleep.

And yet I am happy to be here. Our barracks is like a forbidden city with its bars, its restaurants, its library, its pretty young nurses and its bathrooms with their great wooden tubs. Little Sister and Akiko have sent me books and literary journals, and Mother has really spoiled me with a bag filled to the brim with chocolates, red bean curd, and new socks and underpants.

The pornographic magazines we pass around create a ribald complicity. In the evenings our cracked voices ring out from one room to the next, crucifying traditional Japanese songs. From time to time some of us will meet up for a game of cards where we play for money.

To the despair of the soldiers, the officers are allowed to come and go as they please. Little cliques of party-goers have formed and, as soon as the sun has set, we head out into the town to get drunk and for a post-prandial trip to the brothels.

As I can speak their language, my relationship with the local women takes an unusual turn: the ability to communicate fosters tenderness in even the bitterest heart. Orchid has become very attached to me; I have tamed her physically and she now swears an undying passion for me.

In her imagination this straightforward encounter between a soldier and a prostitute has been turned into a great love story. She claims that she noticed me the very day we first arrived: I was the only one out of all the soldiers streaming through who caught her eye.

She has told me she loves me so many times that I have become faithful to her. She is so ardent and open – not characteristics that our courtesans have at home – that I am enchanted by it. She makes little presents of her handkerchiefs, her socks, locks of her hair and even a little satin cushion embroidered with erotic images. I am just as delighted and flattered by these modest little presents as I am by her frenetic desire.

43

I N MY country the mild and luminous month of May is more fleeting than the leap a frog makes from the bank into the water: summer is already on its way.

The first waves of heat force my parents to take a long nap after lunch. I tiptoe through the house, slip out into the garden and leave by the back gate. I follow winding roads where the trees provide patches of shade as the sun pours its molten gold onto my head. I'm sweating and not thinking about anything.

At Jing's house we are intoxicated by the scent of lilacs. Min is waiting for me in the bed; he has sprinkled himself from head to foot with water from the well. He is icy-cold like a pebble taken from the bottom of a stream. I throw myself at him and my burning skin almost steams as it comes into contact with his.

As I gradually discover Min's body, inch by inch, it becomes an infinite territory that I can explore, listening to the sighs of his skin and reading the map of his veins. Using the tip of my tongue I write characters on his chest and he has to guess what they are. I bring my stomach to his mouth, my breasts to his forehead. Min climbs onto me in a position of prayer and, with every move he makes, he has to recite a poem. His hair tickles me and I laugh, and to punish me for making fun of him, he thrusts hard into me. The whole world is torn open, my eyes go hazy, my ears hum. I bury my fingers in my hair and bite the corner of the sheet. My eyes are half-closed and in the shadows I think I can see bright blocks of colour like flags waving. Contours emerge and disappear, creatures loom out of the dark and melt away again. I am going to die. I suddenly feel as if there are two of me: one part of me leaves my body and floats in the air. She watches me, listens to my moaning and my rasping breath, then rises and disappears into some high unknown place like a bird swooping over a mountain pass, and I can no longer see her.

Min slumps down and goes to sleep with his arm over my breast. He has left a few white droplets on my stomach. They're warm and slip smoothly over my fingers like silk threads. Men are spiders who weave traps for women from their seed.

I get up gently. I am filled with a new energy and I feel ready to embark on a game of go. Jing is snoozing with a straw hat over his face on a chaise longue under a tree in the garden. I don't know when he arrived or whether he watched our exploits. I am just about to leave when he suddenly lifts the hat and stares at me pointedly. I am secretly delighted by the look of despair and contempt I can read in his face, and I meet his eye defiantly. His lips tremble and he can't say a word.

The long drawn-out cries of a fruit vendor reach us.

'I'd like some peaches,' I say.

Jing punches his chair with his fist, gets to his feet and runs off. He comes back with a basket of fruit and cleans them over by the well before choosing the biggest one for me. We eat our peaches in silence. The juice sprays out of Jing's mouth and runs down onto his shirt.

The circadas sing their strident song: the smell of leaves burned by the sun mingles with the smell of my hair. A carp pirouettes in a large jar that serves as an aquarium.

44

AMONG THE new faces at the barracks Captain Nakamura, the information officer, stands out from those who are always keen to find women – he chooses a solitary existence. Despite his rank, he encourages people to make outrageous jokes about him and willingly assumes the role of Kyogen.[1]

In restaurants he usually drinks twenty bottles of *sake* one after the other and then falls asleep and snores loudly. One day we decide to take our revenge on this ostentatiously noisy sleeper: I wake him with a dig of my elbow and start interrogating him like a Zen master talking to his pupil.

'Eating, drinking and seeing women are the vanities of the flesh. Tell me, Captain, what is the vanity of the soul?'

He gets up like a ghost rising from the grave and, oblivious to our laughter, he chants:

---

1 In the theatre of Noh, Kyogens are comic performers who appear between two acts of the play.

> 'The insect cries,
> Growing weaker and quieter,
> The passing of autumn,
> And I, regretting its passing,
> Shall disappear before it . . .

'Yes, the vanity of the soul is death!'

Holding back my smile, I ask him, 'Captain, what is the vanity of vanity?' He is slightly taken aback and scratches his head before replying:

> 'The world in which we live
> is no more real
> than a moonbeam
> reflected in water
> drawn from the palm of the hand . . .'[1]

'The vanity of vanity . . . the vanity of vanity is . . .'

To prolong his torment, I separate out each syllable as I speak: 'Vanity is vain, the vanity of vanities is doubly vain. Now, vanity and vanity cancel each other out. The vanity of the soul is death, the vanity of the vanity of the soul is life. In between life and death, who are we?'

He looks at me and his astonished expression elicits a roar of laughter around us.

When I visit him in his room one afternoon I see a go-set. We start to play a game straight away and, to my great surprise, the Captain who is such an awkward muddler in life plays with considerable ability and with an offhandedness that speaks of confidence. He has earned a reputation as a madman in the barracks because he thinks he sees plots and scheming everywhere, an obsessiveness

1 These two poems are taken from *The Words of Heiji*, a sixteenth-century Japanese novel.

that manifests itself as exaggerated wariness when he plays go.

After his defeat the Captain invites me for dinner, and a few glasses of *sake* are enough to make us the best friends in the world. We talk about Chinese literature and he is amazed that I speak Mandarin. The game of go sets people against each other across the chequered board, but it gives them a reciprocal sense of trust in life. Without any hesitation I open my heart to him.

A woman from Peking followed her student husband to Tokyo. The man died of cancer, leaving her alone in the world with a new-born baby. She spoke only a few words of Japanese and had no money, but she knocked on doors asking for work. Mother took her in as a nanny, she was a gift sent from Buddha. My parents, like all Japanese parents, had given me an implacably strict upbringing: one wrong step and I would get a slap. With cheeks burning, eyes brimming with tears and an aching heart, I would run into the arms of my Chinese nanny and she would weep for me. To wash away my pain she would hug me to her and tell me legends from her homeland. For me, Chinese was the language of dreams and of consolation. Later, she taught me to recite poems from the Tang dynasty and to write. She taught me Confucius's ethics and introduced me to the *Dream of the Red Pavilion*. When I read these out loud, my Peking pronunciation made her sob with joy. She breastfed my brother and sister, and she bewitched us with her gentleness. Then one morning she vanished. A year later Mother destroyed all my illusions: she had gone back to her own country and would never return.

The Captain sighs as he listens to my story. He empties

a glass of *sake*, gets up and, imitating the poses of a Noh actor and using a chopstick as a fan, he sings:

'If he had stayed alive
Nothing would be lost, just lost from sight.
What is the point of living on after him
When, like a tree blowing in the wind,
Sometimes I see him,
Sometimes he disappears,
Fleeting and unsure as ever in this world.
What misery there is in the life of man
Like all the splendour of a flower
Blown by the winds of uncertainty
Which rage all through the night,
Telling us of life and of death,
Covering the unsteady moonlight with clouds.
In truth, to my eyes, the miseries of this world . . .'[1]

I am overcome with sadness and I clap as the Captain bows and empties another glass. Then he changes the subject.

'Did you know that there is a place in the middle of town where the Chinese meet to play go? It's the most incredible sight. Players sit down at tables that have the squares carved onto them, and they wait for someone to come and challenge them. You speak Chinese with such a good Peking accent that you should dress up in civilian clothes and take up their challenge, play a game of go.'

He drinks another glass of *sake* before going on, 'I've been intrigued by this set-up of theirs for a long time, but I've never dared go near them. I don't care how often my informers tell me they're harmless, I'm sure they can't

1 An extract from the Noh play *The Golden Island* by Zeami (1363–1444).

be. Ever since the terrorists managed to get into the town, I keep my eye on everyone, and these people are scheming to bring us down. The game of go is just a camouflage: it's there on that square, as they pretend to play their war game, that our enemies are putting together their twisted strategies.'

The Captain is flushed scarlet and starting to drift into some imaginary universe. I try to sound interested. 'But how could I disguise myself? Would I have to hire a hotel room to get changed in?'

He takes my question seriously. 'This will stay between you and me, I'll cover for you. Tomorrow you can go to one of my men who owns the Chidori restaurant; he'll lend you what you need and he'll tell you how to trick the Chinese, however wary they are. Even though the terrorists have withdrawn from here, their agents are everywhere. They're planning another uprising, but I'll get them this time. Thank you for sacrificing your spare time in the service of the fatherland. Come on, Lieutenant, let's drink to the Emperor.'

I now realise that it was not a joke and it is too late to say no. I empty my glass of *sake* and seal our agreement. The Captain is actually very clever and his quirkiness is deliberate and deceptive. The minute I stepped inside his room he already knew he would use me as a spy. As we played go together, he was setting the trap in which I am now caught: I have no choice but to slip into the skin of a Chinese person.

45

MIN LOATHES games, he thinks they're a waste of time, but this afternoon, after prolonged pleading, I have managed to make him change his mind. He agrees to play cards on condition that we stay in bed and my stomach serves as the table. For him, every pleasure in life is ultimately related to erotic gratification. He is quite incapable of working out his opponent's strategy and loses gloriously, rushing to throw his cards down between my breasts. I find his laziness and his flippant attitude exasperating and, to punish him, I leave the room on some flimsy pretext and head off to the Square of a Thousand Winds.

The players are sitting there meditating and snoozing. Having failed to find a partner, I sit myself down at a table and wait for an amateur player to come past. With my head resting on one hand, I lay out the stones and start an imaginary game against Min. A shadow falls over me and I look up. A stranger, with a panama hat pushed right down over his tortoiseshell-rimmed glasses, inclines his head slightly. I reply with a nod and gesture towards the chair opposite me. The Stranger doesn't seem to understand and makes as if to move away, but I stop him.

'Do you know how to play go?'

He still doesn't speak.

'Come on, you look like a connoisseur. Sit down, let's play.'

'May I ask at what level you play?' the lump asks me with a terrible Peking accent.

'I don't know.'

'I don't want to play without some knowledge of your handicap.'

'Let's start a game. I'll give you a little demonstration!'

He hesitates for a moment and eventually sits down opposite me. It's obvious that this stranger has no idea of my reputation. Like a lot of stupid people, he is deceived by my appearance.

I push the black stones towards him noisily.

'Over to you.'[1]

He puts his first stone down in the north-west corner. His pretentious behaviour earlier is still niggling at me and I decide to play a nasty trick on him. I reply by sticking a white stone alongside it. You never start the battle with such close combat at the beginning of a game. That is one of the golden rules.

Disconcerted, he looks up at me and sinks into thought for a long time.

The stones fight over the 361 intersections formed between the nineteen horizontal lines and the nineteen vertical lines on the square board. The two players divide up this virgin land and, at the end, compare the extent of

---

1 In the game of go the black stones begin the game, but they have to concede 5½ points to the whites in the count-up when the game is over.

their occupied territories. I prefer go to chess because it is so much freer: in a game of chess the two kingdoms with their armoured warriors confront each other across the board, but the agile, twirling stones in a game of go spiral round each other, setting traps – daring and imagination are the qualities that lead to victory.

Instead of establishing my frontiers, I attack my opponent head-on. My white number four lures him into a duel. He stops to think again.

My number six is blocking his black number five, and rallies with the others to surround his number one.

In extremis, he parries by placing his number seven.

I smile. The joke is over, now I am constructing my game.

The Stranger plays infinitely slowly. I am surprised by his convoluted deliberations: each of his moves translates a desire for harmony within the whole. His stones make a subtle, airborne sort of progress like the dance of the cranes. I didn't know that in Peking there was a school where elegance had the edge over violence. Now it is my turn to be perplexed, and I let myself be carried away by his rhythm.

The Stranger suddenly interrupts the game just when it is becoming really exciting.

'I have a meeting,' he says gruffly.

A little put out and wanting to resume the game as soon as possible, I say, 'Come back at ten o'clock on Sunday morning.'

Through his glasses I can see that there still isn't a glimmer of enthusiasm in his eyes.

'Never mind, then,' I say, standing up.

'All right,' he agrees eventually.

I make a note of the positions of the stones on a piece

of paper and gratify the Stranger with a smile. Having used it on Cousin Lu, Min and Jing, I know my weapon well.

And he does indeed look away.

46

THE DISGUISE I have chosen – a linen tunic, a panama hat and a fan embellished with calligraphy – gives something of the solemnity of an imperial official to my character, and a pair of glasses makes him look like an academic.

The rickshaw boy can tell straight away that I am not from the area, and he decides to swindle me: instead of going straight to the Square of a Thousand Winds, he sets off on a long detour round the town. His voice shuddering with the physical effort, he tells me some of the history of the region. Four hundred years ago the court nobles discovered the local forest and built sumptuous palaces on its fringes. For many centuries they cherished these lands, which were rich in game and beautiful women. A Thousand Winds, which was originally just a small village, grew into a town where trade and local crafts could flourish. The city is like a miniature copy of Peking and has copied its rectangular layout. When the Manchurian Empire disintegrated, some of the Peking aristocracy followed the Emperor to the New Capital; others took refuge here. They can be identified by their elegant brand of poverty: they wear outdated robes, and they oppose any form of modernity by keeping their nails long (a sign of the leisured classes) and their heads shaved with the traditional little plait at the back.

After taking me along the ramparts, which are seething with beggars, fire-breathers and monkey trainers, and after showing me the main square with its large, old-fashioned private houses, he eventually comes to a stop on the edge of a wooded square.

'This is the Square of a Thousand Winds,' he says and then asks mysteriously, 'Do you play too?'

I do not answer.

All round the park players confront each other in silence across the low tables, and judging by their clothes they come from all levels of society. If I had not come here I would never have believed such a place existed where a passer by could be offered a game of go. I have always thought that go was reserved exclusively for an élite, and that each game was a ceremony carried out with the greatest of respect.

I do not find this phenomenon surprising, though. According to legend, this extraordinary game was invented by the Chinese 4,000 years ago, but during the course of its over-long history, its traditions have been worn away, and the game has lost its air of refinement and the purity of its origins. Go was introduced to Japan over a thousand years ago and there it has been meditated over and perfected to the point of becoming a divine art. Once again, my country has demonstrated its superiority over China.

In the distance I can see a young woman busy playing against herself. At home it would be unthinkable for a woman to be alone in a place where there are so many men. Intrigued, I move closer.

She is younger than I thought she was, and she is wearing a school dress. She is sitting with her head resting in the hollow of her hand, deep in thought. The stones have been laid out on the board with considerable skill, and they draw me in to examine them more closely.

She looks up, wide forehead and slanting eyes like two finely drawn willow leaves. It is as if I am looking at Sunlight aged sixteen, but the illusion is short-lived: the apprentice geisha had a shy, closed sort of beauty, but this Chinese girl sits watching me unabashed. At home, elegance is associated with pallor and women avoid the sun; this girl has spent so much time playing outside that her face glows with a strange charm. Her eyes meet mine before I can look away.

She invites me to a game of go, and I pretend to hesitate to make my character more believable. Before I left the Chidori restaurant, Captain Nakamura's collaborator told me that over the last ten years my country has become a window on the Western world for the whole of Asia. If I claim to be one of those Chinese students who has spent a long time in Tokyo, that will justify my manner, my accent and my ignorance on some topical issues.

The Chinese girl does not like talking much; she does not ask me a single question and urges me to start. With her very first move she establishes a perverse and extravagant strategy. I have never played go with a woman; I have never been so close to one except for my mother, my sister, Akiko, geishas and prostitutes. Even though the chequered table-top lies between me and my opponent, the young-girl smell of her makes me feel uncomfortable.

She looks as if she is dreaming as she tilts her head to one side, completely absorbed in her thoughts. Her soft face contrasts sharply with her prickly manoeuvres – I find her intriguing.

How old is she? Sixteen? Seventeen? With her flat chest and her two plaits, she has all the ambiguity of adolescence, which makes girls look like transvestite boys. And yet the first signs of femininity are just emerging, like snowdrops in early spring: there is an indolent roundness to her forearms.

Night is falling quickly now and I have to get back to the barracks. She invites me to come again, and this invitation from any other woman would be somehow immodest, but this young girl knows how to put her innocence to good use.

I do not answer. She puts the stones away in their pot, clattering them against each other, a racket that is clearly a protest against my indifference. I laugh inwardly: she would be a great player if she could moderate her aggression and apply herself to a more spiritual path.

'Ten o'clock on Sunday morning,' she says.

I like her perseverance: I offer no further resistance, and agree with a nod of the head.

At home, when women laugh they hide their faces behind the sleeves of their kimonos. The Chinese girl smiles without any embarrassment or artifice. Her mouth opens with all the irresistible power of a grenade exploding.

I look away.

47

A GROUP of pilgrims walks along an apparently endless wall and, finding a breach, they step into the enclosed area. Inside there are thousands of trees around a sparkling, rippling lake. A child is playing with a kite inside a ruined pavilion.

He smiles maliciously at the pilgrims and greets them, telling them that his kite can predict the future.

'Does it know where we are going?' asks the oldest member of the group.

The kite flies off towards a corner of the ceiling, then changes direction and hurtles towards the opposite corner. Like a bird trapped in a cage, it flaps against the walls, crashes into the windows and suddenly plummets to the ground.

'Into the Darkness!'

I wake up.

This morning Min catches up with my rickshaw on his bicycle and stuffs a book into my hand. I leaf through it and find a note folded into four. He is inviting me over to Jing's house at the end of the afternoon to celebrate his friend's twentieth birthday. I decide to introduce Huong to Jing – their meeting can be my birthday present.

In the garden of Jing's house there are students smoking, drinking and chatting. The boys are there with their white silk scarves round their necks, posturing like tragic poets. With their flat shoes and their short hair, the girls are more masculine than their male companions. One of the girls is in the centre of the gathering, haranguing her fellow students, and Min is leaning up against a tree, listening attentively. From time to time he casts his eye over the crowd, but doesn't see me.

Jing comes out of the house and puts a tray of tea down on a stool. I introduce him to Huong, who is intrigued by these young revolutionaries, and they launch into an animated conversation.

I flop down onto a chair and, to shrug off my boredom, I split open salted sunflower seeds as I watch the student girl talking. I surprise myself by finding her pretty despite her fierce, indomitable manner. She is only twenty, but she is an orator, she knows how to modulate her voice and to keep her listeners' attention. With each of her words I am gripped by a devastating admiration for her.

'Japan is in the throes of massive military expansion, it's not going to be satisfied with colonising Manchuria; the next step will be Peking, then Shanghai and Guang Dong. The sovereignty of China is at risk! Soon we shall be servants, slaves, stray dogs! The war-lords, the provisional governments and the military authorities have carved up our continent. Only patriotism can unite our strength and hope. We must rebel, we must expel these invaders and exterminate the corrupt soldiers who thirst for the blood of our people. We must give the land back to the peasants, we must give the serfs back their dignity. Let us build on the ruins of this semi-feudal, semi-colonial regime; let us build a new China where democracy reigns, where there is no corruption, no poverty and no violence. Equality, freedom and fraternity – that will be our motto. Every citizen shall work according to his needs. The people will be masters, and the government will be at their service. Only then will we know peace and happiness again!'

People clap and, having waved to her admirers, she turns towards Min. The hard glint in her eye gives way to gentleness, and he responds with a smile. I get up and go over to join Jing and Huong. She is exercising her charms on him, talking about her family and her arranged marriage. She is watching him with unbearable intensity and he is fascinated, he can't take his eyes off her. His face reflects curiosity and pity in turn. The fact that I am there makes him feel uncomfortable; he keeps glancing towards me and when he catches my eye he looks away, gives a little cough and resumes his haughty expression.

I wander round the garden, but I can't shake off the crushing pain inside me. There are red dragonflies alighting on flower stems and flitting away in the last rays of sunlight. Through the bedroom window I can see the bed I lay in just yesterday, covered in that same crimson sheet embroidered with chrysanthemums. The sight of it hurts me.

Min waves to me. At last. In front of his friends he treats me like a little sister and laughs as he tells them how he saved my life. I let him crow; he is ashamed of me.

Jing has just started handing round the birthday biscuits. When it is my turn, instead of offering the plate to me, he stops and takes a leaf that has caught in my hair.

Someone taps him on the shoulder and says, 'Will you introduce me to your friend?'

I recognise the prophetess from earlier. She doesn't wait for a response from Jing and addresses me directly.

'Hello, my name is Tang,' she says and goes on to ask me so many questions so quickly that I feel intimidated. She wants to know everything: where I go to school, where I live, how many brothers and sisters I have. Then, without a whisper of embarrassment, she lets me know that she has known my lover all her life – her mother works for Min's family. She scribbles her address on a piece of paper and invites me to go round and see her.

I tell them that I am expected back at home, entrust Huong to Jing's tender care and leave the party. Jing catches up with me on the doorstep, puts his hands on the doorjambs to block my way and thanks me for coming. He suddenly flushes scarlet and I realise that he really likes Huong. I feel peculiarly annoyed.

'Go back to the party. They're waiting for you.'

In my pocket I find the handkerchief he wiped himself with the day he took me home on his bicycle. I take it out. I have cleaned it and embroidered his name on it.

'Here, a little present.'

Jing looks at the handkerchief and stammers, 'I'm so glad I've met you. You're special, you're interesting . . . Min doesn't deserve you . . .'

I ask him why and he stares right at me, biting his lower lip. I ask again, but he stamps his foot angrily and turns away.

It is hot and humid out in the street. The trees shine with moisture and the green drips from the ends of the leaves. The shop windows scatter their haphazard glints of the failing sun. Children run almost naked along the pavements, brandishing newspapers. To attract customers, they chorus: 'Woman kills her lover! Body found by Buddhist priest!'

Just before I reach the house, Min suddenly appears and catches hold of my arms to stop me.

'Jing's gone mad! What did he say to you earlier?'

'Nothing.'

'What did he say about me?'

'Nothing.'

Min is still not reassured, and he looks at me closely.

'He loves you,' he says, 'he's just told me', and his words seem to pierce my heart.

'Leave me alone,' I say quietly.

'You'll have to choose between us.'

'Oh, don't let's make such a scene!'

'You can't betray me. Your body belongs to me!'

'I'm free. I can give my body to whoever I like, even the devil!'

'Why did you say that? Why do you want to hurt me? You don't love me!'

'Leave me alone,' I say again, 'my sister's waiting for me at home, I'll talk to you when you've calmed down. Tomorrow I'm playing a game of go on the Square of a Thousand Winds. Come and pick me up at five o'clock.'

I have never seen Min in such a state: he is trembling from head to foot, and I run off to get away from him.

48

AFTER DINNER we are ordered to sleep fully clothed, weapons to hand. At midnight we are woken by sharp blows of a whistle and I race outside.

Our unit divides into several sections and dives into lorries. We are told that the object of this operation is to arrest a group of terrorists who have gathered in the town this evening. We think that the infamous Colonel Li may be among them.

It is a heavy, humid night. Geometrid moths flap under the street lights. In the wealthiest, most respected district there are oil lamps lighting the imposing gateways. Suddenly there is a burst of gunfire. The terrorists know they are being cornered and are trying to escape; our scouts have opened fire on them.

A grenade goes off in a nearby road, and the smell of the powder makes me shudder. It is months since I have taken part in a battle: I have missed that sense of death.

We surround a huge residence. The rebels are inside, crouching below the windows, resisting our attack by throwing grenades. There are trees burning where their projectiles have fallen. The windows with their shattered panes are dark as the mouths of animals' lairs.

The assaults made by our section have allowed one of our commandos to get up onto the roof, where he finds an opening. The fighting is over too quickly: I am only just warming up and I have to lower my weapon. The terrorists leave behind five bodies and eight wounded. The famous rebel colonel had the wisdom to take his own life before we broke in. There is a lot to plunder: in the cellars there are piles of rifles, cases of ammunition and wodges of Chinese currency that the terrorists have not had time to change into Manchurian money. We intervened just in time – a new insurrection was about to explode.

I count our losses: four soldiers and one officer have left their lives for the Emperor of Japan. There is something moving by the doorway of a nearby house: a soldier, hit by a grenade, is crawling along the pavement, taking long, agonising breaths. His body is reduced to great chunks of mangled flesh, churned up with the shreds of his clothes. His entrails spew from his open belly. He gets hold of me suddenly and says, 'Go on, kill me!'

I know that he has had it. I know that this is how soldiers die, but I cannot bring myself to take my pistol from its holster.

'Kill me, you bastard! What are you waiting for?'

I am not strong enough. I stand there with my hand on my pistol, feeling light-headed. The ambulance men run over and carry the injured man off on a stretcher, but he still keeps on yelling, 'Kill me! I beg you, please! Kill me!'

Back at the barracks I collapse onto my bed without undressing. The sleeves of my uniform are still wet with the blood of this stranger, who will die slowly and painfully in hospital. His despair is haunting. I could not give him the gift of death, I was weak, a coward. Buddha would have committed the crime of deliverance. Compassion belongs to those who have strength in their souls.

My mother's words ring in my ears: 'If you have to choose between death and cowardice, don't hesitate: choose death.'

49

I WATCH the moon through the window and the trees outside. In my mind, I see Jing again with his hands on the doorposts and a strange gleam in his eye. He is thanking me for coming.

He has seemed wild and aloof for such a long time, and I haven't dared to tease him once without worrying about his moody temper. Now that I have had this confession, via Min, I am no longer afraid of his apparent disdain. He is like an open book to me: I could write every word of him.

Why did Jing say that Min didn't deserve me? How did the two of them end up confronting each other? What persuaded Jing suddenly to make his confession? Did they have an argument? Did they fight?

Min says he wants to marry me, but I am afraid that he will eventually be like my father and my brother-in-law. A man's passion wanes more quickly than a woman's beauty.

He asked me to choose, but how could I stop seeing Jing who feeds my attraction to Min? I can't betray Min, he made me a woman; it is my gratitude, and not his jealousy, which makes me faithful. My relationship with Jing is more subtle than any physical excitement . . . abstinence is the sensuous pleasure of the soul. I know that Jing is watching us, that he is experiencing with me the dazzling discovery of the pleasures of the flesh, and when I look at him all his resentment melts away. When I turn to him, his pale face fills with all the colour of life again: he is my child, my brother with whom all physical contact is forbidden. This purity is the beginning of a boundless and defenceless affection that I can't bring myself to give to Min.

Without Jing, my couplings with his rival would somehow become vulgar. Without Min, Jing no longer exists. Compared to my lover's flippancy, his arid character seems serious and full of mystery. If I choose one I would have to forgo the other, and I would lose them both.

In this sort of situation in a game of go, the player opts for a third solution: attacking the opponent where he least expects it. When Min comes to get me on the Square of a Thousand Winds tomorrow I will pretend not to see him. When the game is over I will count up the stones, bid goodbye to my opponent and watch him walk away until he has disappeared. I will stare at the chequered table-top as if I am exhausted and then I will ask, 'Min, who is Tang?'

He will swear he is faithful to me. I will pretend to be angry, I will stamp my feet and sigh – I remember Moon Pearl's cries so clearly that I will play the part to perfection.

To calm me down he will take me to Jing's house. I will accept his kisses, he will climb on top of me, our two bodies will be wrapped in the crimson sheet like two pine trees bound together by ivy. The bed will be our palanquin, carrying us off to another world.

A deafening sound wakes me from my dreams. Looking out of the window I can see my parents in their pyjamas out in the courtyard. The cook has been woken too and has come out of her room with a candle in her hand.

'Put it out!' my father orders her in a hoarse whisper.

'I hope it's just a military exercise,' says Mother.

Father sighs.

There are more explosions, they sound like the firecrackers that go off when we celebrate the beginning of spring. Our town counters the explosive din with a stubborn silence: not one footstep, not a single whisper or a sob.

Then everything goes back to the normality of a starlit night. My parents return to their bedroom and the cook shuts the door.

The moon watches us, motionless.

50

A s soon as dawn breaks we run tirelessly round the three-kilometre perimeter of the barracks. Our rhythmic footfalls send up clouds of dust and our patriotic songs ring out between the earth and the sky. Our collective enthusiasm warms the heart and dissipates nightmares.

Last night I was wandering through the ruins left by the earthquake. The sky was black with smoke. My ears had become so accustomed to the sobbing that they could no longer distinguish between people crying and insects buzzing. I was exhausted and I would have liked to stop and rest, but every inch of ground was splattered with blood. I stumbled with every step, cursing the gods and shouting imprecations that still rang in my ears after I woke up.

In the bathhouse my fellow officers spend hours in front of the mirrors shaving so that their moustaches are perfectly squared off. I splash my head with ice-cold water and turn to face the mirror. When my image appears I instinctively look away.

Is there a truth on the other side that we do not want to see?

I hold my breath as I look at myself, with my hair standing up in tufts and my bushy eyebrows. My bad night's sleep has injected red into the whites of my eyes. I examine my naked torso: my skin is red and steaming from the run; there are thick veins running up my neck; the muscles stand proud on my arms; there is a long scar along my left shoulder, a reminder of a bayonet exercise in which I was injured. The twenty-four years of my life have flown by. Who am I? I cannot find an answer. But at least I know why I am alive: my body, which is now ripe, and my mind, which has doubted, loved and then believed, will be my gift – like a cluster of fireworks – to the party. I will explode on the night of our victory.

A quarter to ten and I am knocking at the door of the Chidori. The manager makes me put on my disguise and, as a Mandarin, I slip out of a secret door and into the street.

Seen from my rickshaw, the town still looks incredibly calm. Along the pavements the nonchalance of the Chinese contrasts with our soldiers' slick marching as they move about in square formations. The shops have opened their doors and the traders have set up their stalls. The tireless street vendors intone their litanies. I ask the rickshaw boy whether he was woken by the firing in the night, but he pretends not to hear me.

On the Square of a Thousand Winds the players remain faithful to habit and have started their games. I keep half an ear on their conversations, but they only open their mouths to comment on the game.

The Chinese girl appears on the edge of the wood and

runs over to our table, light as a bird. There are beads of sweat on her brow.

'I'm sorry,' she says as she sits down.

She unties a bundle of blue cotton cloth and hands me the lacquered pot with the black stones in it.

'Go on. It's your turn.'

I am perplexed by the indifference these people seem to be displaying to last night's incidents.

51

WHEN I woke up this morning the sun had already reached the top of the pear tree. The sprigs of new leaves on every branch look like flowers lolling open.

I am happy, but this happiness doesn't draw on a feeling of peace, it is fed by contradictory emotions. The cicadas, acutely aware of the secrets of my soul, chant gleefully. The light of a pale sky spills onto my bed through the open curtains. I imagine my town, offered up to the light, as a naked woman waiting for her lover's embrace.

Mother has gone to the market with my sister. Father has shut himself in the library where he battles assiduously with Shakespeare's language. The house is cool and calm, the doors and windows stand open and the smell of leaves mingles with the heady fragrance of jasmine that permeates our rooms. In the sitting room Wang Ma, the maid, is busy with a feather duster.

The poor woman's son died of tuberculosis six months ago. She goes over and over the memories of him, and the dead boy is now more alive than ever. Father listens to her – while he goes on thinking about his books – and comforts her with some completely meaningless phrase: 'You must have strength, my dear.' She can communicate her pain more easily to Mother and Moon Pearl. Her endless reminiscences elicit their sighs and sometimes even tears.

This morning my feeling of compassion has changed to uneasiness. I am carrying my happiness in my belly as if I were pregnant, and I don't want it to be ruined by Wang Ma's sobbing, not at any cost. Before she even opens her mouth, I rush outside.

'I'm going to the Square of a Thousand Winds,' I say. 'I'll be back later.'

The Stranger is already waiting for me. His face is hidden by his glasses, but I can see that it is stiff and motionless like his body. Sitting bolt upright on his stool, he looks like a guard at the gates of hell in some ancient temple.

We position our soldiers at the intersections. The Stranger delimits his territories on the outer edges of the chequerboard with prodigious precision and economy. Go reflects the soul: his is meticulous and cold.

My generosity in letting him play first gives him an advantage: he is one step ahead of me in occupying the strategic positions. Disputing these with him would disadvantage me further. I decide to take a risk: sure of my base in the north-west corner, I set out to conquer the centre.

It is hot and I flap my fan back and forth in vain. I am impressed by my opponent: he sits opposite me, exposed to the sun, and lets it burn down on him without showing any sign of irritation. He sits completely motionless, his face streaming with sweat, his hands on his knees and his fan held tightly closed.

The sun is reaching its highest point. I ask to break for lunch and make a note of our positions on a piece of paper. We agree to meet after the pause.

52

THE CHINESE girl has gone home for lunch and I choose a Korean restaurant that seems to have very few customers. I order cold noodles, and sit in a corner overlooking the whole room so that I can keep an eye on the comings and goings of the waiters as I write the beginnings of a letter to my mother.

I tell her what I need: soap, towels, newspapers, books and bean-curd cakes. My years spent at the military academy made a man of me, but my time spent far from my homeland has turned me into a capricious child. I insist on particular brands, giving details of the colour and the flavour. I rewrite the list twenty times and my raging nostalgia eventually calms.

How are the flowers in the garden? How is Little Brother, who has been called up by the army? Does he come home once a month? Do they give him a good meal and warm *sake*? What is my Little Sister doing as I think about her now? What is the weather like in Tokyo?

Everyone knows that mail can be intercepted and monitored and so, for fear of betraying military secrets, our soldiers' letters to their families are excruciatingly bland. The replies are in the same vein. When we are gone, will the fact that we do not complain or express our fears make us look like intrepid heroes?

I pull to pieces every sentence from Japan, and my family have their own way of interpreting my words to them. Fearing that she might weaken my will, Mother has never said in her letters that she misses me. So as not to make her cry, I have never told her how I suffer from being away from my country.

Only the vocabulary of death is allowed between us. She writes, 'Do not hesitate to die to honour the Emperor. It is the path of your fate.' And I reply, 'What joy to sacrifice myself for my beloved country.' I will not tell her that I shall also die for her glory, and she will never admit that my death will destroy her.

I end my letter by saying, 'According to Confucius, "a man who knows humanity will never agree to preserve his life at the expense of that humanity". This courageous virtue has become the key to my very existence. Pray, venerable Mother, I beg you, that I may soon attain this ideal.'

53

A<small>T HOME</small> lunch is served in the big sitting room where the shutters have been kept closed to preserve the cool of morning. My sister has come back from market, and tells us the news she has gleaned.

She informs us that last night the Japanese army arrested some members of the Resistance Movement who were secretly planning an insurrection. The firing we heard came not from an exercise, but from true carnage.

I listen to her half-heartedly; when I am in the middle of a game of go, it completely intoxicates me and cuts me off from the outside world. The darkness of the sitting room reminds me of the bedroom at Jing's house, shadowy as an imperial tomb: where the black lacquered furniture exhales a heavy scent and the cracks in the walls form mysterious frescos. The bed covered in crimson silk embroidered with gold is an eternal fire.

'An insurrection,' my sister is saying. 'Don't you see! How stupid!' she exclaims, and then she goes on, 'Do you know where the would-be rioters were arrested? Wait for it: the mayor's own son had got them together in one of his houses. Don't look at me as if I'm making it all up. Apparently they found guns and cases of ammunition in the cellar. What? Of course they arrested him.'

The chicken I am eating suddenly tastes of nothing. To get it down I fill my mouth with rice, but I can't swallow it.

The cook who is serving tea intervenes with 'At dawn this morning the Japanese arrested Doctor Li. He was one of the conspirators.'

Father speaks up slowly.

'I knew the mayor well. Our fathers served together in the Dowager Empress's court. We saw a great deal of each other in our youth. He wanted to go to England to study, but his family wouldn't let him. It's something he has always regretted. The other day he came to say hello to me after my conference. Now that he's fifty he looks just like his father – all he needs is the hat with the peacock feathers, the coral necklaces and the brocade tunics. As he shook my hand he told me that his elder brother, a close adviser to the Emperor of Manchuria, had found a post for him at court in the New Capital. His career will be ruined now, and I fear for his life and his family's future.'

'How can you feel sorry for that man,' Mother retorts. 'He loathes us. When he was adviser to the previous mayor, he schemed to have your teaching hours reduced. I suspect he even tried to have your translations banned. I haven't forgotten anything, and I don't care if he's in trouble now.'

I didn't know that my parents knew Jing's father, and I am devastated by what they are saying – there they are sitting round the table in the half-light, commenting on all this as if it was just a gang of troublemakers who had been arrested.

'Why are you looking at me like that?' my sister asks suddenly.

'I've got a stomach ache.'

'You don't look well. Go and lie down,' says my mother. 'We'll send some tea up for you.'

I lie down on the bed and put my ice-cold hands over my stomach.

Where is Jing? Is Min with him? I can see each crack in the wall, every piece of furniture and every ornament in that house. They seem worn and peaceful, there isn't the tiniest suggestion of revolt in them. And yet my friends managed to fool me. When Min put his arms round me and led me off to the bedroom, he was walking over the secrets in the cellar. When Jing talked to me in the garden and spied jealously on Min, there was a link far stronger than love between him and his friend. Why did they hide the truth from me? I would have joined them in their patriotic fervour, I would have gone to prison, I would have died beside them. Why did they seduce me only to exclude me?

My sister brings me a cup of tea. I turn towards the wall and pretend to be asleep.

I remember the first time we met: the Resistance had launched their attack on the town hall. I was jostled by the crowd, I fell and a dark-skinned boy held out his hand to me. He had the fine, square face of the Manchurian aristocracy. Then there was Jing, cold and aloof. The two people who had organised the revolt had just come into my life.

I roll over, take a few good sips of tea and begin to calm down. When Min talked about the revolution I thought he was dreaming. When he told me his life was dangerous, I made fun of his taste for adventure.

I remember Tang, the student girl who was invited to Jing's birthday. Now I understand the importance of what she was saying: she was the daughter of a slave and she had found her strength and confidence in the Communist ideal. The Japanese invasion broke down our immutable hierarchies, and now Tang could communicate to Min – who was young, landed and noble – the dream of building a new society where all men would be equal. She persuaded him to take up arms and sign up to the Resistance Movement. And Min had dragged Jing into it. They would be shot, all three of them!

I slip out. The rickshaw takes me past Jing's house, but the road is barred by guards.

On the Square of a Thousand Winds I lay out the stones in the positions I noted earlier. I stare at the chequered pattern and count the intersections, sinking into the oblivion of mathematics.

54

THE CHINESE girl's face is pale after lunch, her features altered. When she reaches for one of the stones her hand shakes. She is silent, forbidding me to comfort her. I affect indifference so as not to distress her; she would not want to be pitied.

She seems to have aged several years in the space of a few hours. Her cheekbones are heightened by the shadows carved across her cheeks. Her face looks longer, her chin more angular.

For a moment I glimpse the terrible pain of a child whose pride has been wounded. Has she had a row with a brother? Fallen out with one of her girlfriends? She will get over it, I should not worry about her. Girls' moods change very quickly and she will soon be smiling again.

During the previous session she struck me as being a quick and spontaneous player, but today she is deliberating for hours. With her eyes lowered and her lips clamped into a hard line, she could serve as a model for the mask of a ghost woman in the theatre of Noh.

She looks exhausted sitting there with her elbows on the edge of the table and her head resting in her palms. I wonder whether she is really thinking about the game. The stones betray our thoughts. One more intersection to the east and her strike would have been more substantial.

My black stone falls in alongside her. By responding aggressively I am hoping to break through her vigilance. She looks up. I think she is going to cry, but she smiles.

'Well played! Let's meet up again tomorrow afternoon.'

I would like to carry on now, but as a matter of principle I never argue with a woman.

She makes a note of our latest moves on her piece of paper. If a game has to be interrupted during tournaments in Japan, the judge makes a note of the positions and, in front of everyone, puts this note carefully into a locked safe.

'Would you like it?' she asks me.

'No, keep it, please.'

She looks at me for a long time, and puts her stones away.

55

MIN IS clearly silhouetted against the sky at the far end of the street. I have been waiting at the crossroads for hours and now, as he finally cycles towards me, he greets me with a nod of his head. I can't take my eyes off him. His face is smooth and doesn't betray any sign of suffering. The sweat gleams on his forehead as he smiles at me and cycles on.

I must find Jing! I get through the cordon of Japanese soldiers and go into his house. Inside its crumbling walls the house is riddled with bullet-holes, and in the garden only the crimson dahlias still hold their heads high. Jing is lying on a chaise longue playing with his bird.

'I thought you were in prison.'

He looks up, his eyes filled with hate and desire.

'You are my prison.'

I wake up.

From daybreak the crossroads in front of the temple is full of traders, people out for a morning walk and Taoist monks. I sit in front of a stall and force myself to have some ravioli soup. Through the steam rising from the boiling pot, I watch for Min.

People wander past, rickshaw boys wear themselves out. Where are they going? Do they have sons and brothers who have been taken prisoner by the Japanese? I envy the Taoist monks their detachment, the tiny children their ignorance and the beggars their uncomplicated misery. When a bicycle appears on the horizon I get up anxiously. For the first time I understand why people talk about keeping their eyes 'peeled'.

Soon the sun is three-quarters of the way up its celestial trajectory, and I slip under a willow tree. There are Japanese soldiers marching over the crossroads with flags fixed to their bayonets. I can make out their cruel young faces under their helmets. Short and stocky with deep slits for eyes and squashed noses above their moustaches, they are the very incarnation of their insular people who, according to legend, are descended from our own. I find them disgusting.

At eleven o'clock I decide to go to school. Huong tells me that our literature teacher noticed I wasn't there and made a note of my name.

'Why are you late?' she asks, and I tell her what has happened.

She thinks about it and then says, 'You should disappear for a while. You saw a lot of Min and Jing – the Japanese could take an interest in you.'

She makes me laugh.

'If they come to look for me,' I say, 'I'd gladly give myself up. Where can I hide? If I run away my parents will be sent to prison instead of me. Let them arrest me if that's what they want!'

Huong begs me not to do anything stupid.

'I won't do anything. I'm too sensible and too weak. I'm never going to go and set fire to the Japanese barracks

159

to save my friends. They're true heroes. They know how to fire a pistol, throw grenades and set dynamite to explode. They know how to risk their lives for something they believe in. But I've never even touched a weapon. I don't know what they feel like or how they work. I didn't even recognise members of the Resistance when I met them. I'm just so ordinary.'

56

CAPTAIN NAKAMURA sees spies everywhere, even within our own army. Unsure how accurate the Chinese interpreters are, he begs me to attend the interrogations of our new prisoners.

The cells are in a courtyard in the middle of the barracks, hidden under tall plane trees. I have scarcely set foot through the door when I am hit by the same stench as a battlefield the day after combat.

I am welcomed with open arms by Lieutenant Oka, whom Captain Nakamura has already introduced to me at dinner once in town. His uniform is made to measure, his moustache impeccable; this is a man who attaches excessive importance to his appearance.

He takes me over to a second courtyard where a Chinese man is hanging from the branch of a tree by his feet. His naked body is criss-crossed with black marks. As we move closer a cloud of flies rises to reveal his flesh, which looks as if it has been ploughed like a field.

'After I whipped him, I used a white-hot iron on him,' commented the Lieutenant.

The smell of decomposition intensifies inside the

building, but Lieutenant Oka seems unperturbed and I force myself to ignore it too. He offers me a guided tour, and he shows me the cells along a long, dark corridor with all the relaxed confidence of a doctor proud of his model hospital. Through the bars I can make out mutilated bodies slumped on the ground. The Lieutenant explains that the first thing he did when he arrived was to have the ceilings lowered so that the criminals could not stand upright; then he cut their food rations.

I am suffocated by the smell of excrement and blood and, noticing my discomfort, my guide manages to sound like a conscientious civil servant: 'I'm so sorry, Lieutenant, when we hit these pigs with sticks they go and get diarrhoea.'

Seeing these men dying in agony makes my skin crawl with goose pimples, but the Lieutenant's serene and attentive expression means that I have to hide my disgust. I must not show any lack of respect for his work and, afraid that he might make fun of my weak stomach, I choke back the bile rising in my throat and make a few complimentary remarks. He seems satisfied and smiles shyly.

The torture rooms are at the end of the corridor; the Lieutenant put them there deliberately so that the cries of the tortured prisoners could ring throughout the entire building. Keen to show off his expertise to me, he tells his adjutant to carry on with an interrogation.

I hear a woman screaming and it makes the hair on my head stand up.

'They've just put salt in the Communist's wounds,' the Lieutenant explains. 'When I was in training our instructors would often say that under torture women show more resistance than men. This one is especially stubborn.'

He pushes a door open: in the middle of the room there is a fire blazing in a bronze basin, heating pokers till they glow red. The heat is unbearable. Two torturers with great hairy arms throw a bucket of water over a woman lying naked on the floor.

The Chinese interpreter bends over her and cries, 'Talk! If you talk, the imperial army will leave you with your life.'

Between her moans I think I can make out the words: 'Go to the devil, you Japanese dogs.'

'What is she saying?' asks Lieutenant Oka.

'She is insulting the gentlemen of the imperial army.'

'Tell her that her friends have confessed. She's the only one who's not co-operating. What point is there in resisting?'

She curls up on her stomach with her hands tied behind her back, which shudders as she moves. The Lieutenant kicks her and, as she jerks onto her side, I see her face, which is blue and swollen.

He crushes her head with his boot and smiles.

'Tell her that if she doesn't talk, I'll ram this poker up her arse.'

The interpreter quickly does as he is told. The moaning stops. All our eyes are riveted on the motionless figure. The Lieutenant gives a signal to the interpreter, who picks up a pen and a piece of paper. Suddenly the woman gets up to her knees, like a fury rising from the depths of hell, and she starts screaming, 'Kill me! Kill me! You're all damned . . .'

The Lieutenant doesn't need the interpreter to grasp the gist of what she is saying. He only has to glance at the two torturers and they throw themselves at the woman and hold her by her shoulders. The Lieutenant grabs the glowing iron.

A foul-smelling smoke rises up into the air at the same time as the tortured woman's scream. I look away. The Lieutenant puts the iron back into the fire and stares at me with an enigmatic smile.

'Stop for now. We'll start again later.'

He takes me off to see other rooms and comments on the hooks, whips, sticks, needles, boiling oil, and water spiced with red-hot chillies, with all the minute detail of an impassioned scientist. Then he offers me a glass of *sake* in his office.

'I'm sorry, I never drink during the day.'

He bursts out laughing.

'A prison is always a kingdom in its own right. We make our own laws here. *Sake* activates the brain. Without it our imaginations would run dry and we'd soon be exhausted.'

I take my leave, claiming that I am nearly late for a meeting. On the doorstep he says, 'You will come back soon, won't you?'

I nod vaguely in his direction.

Back in my room, I write my report for Captain Nakamura, and in it I praise Lieutenant Oka: 'He is a meticulous man who is devoted to the Emperor. He must be left to act as he sees fit and with the complete co-operation of his assistants. An outsider would disrupt the precision of his work and would interfere with the smooth running of the interrogations. I myself would ask you not to send me there again, Captain. My visit there underlined my conviction that we should never fall into enemy hands alive.'

Three days later a soldier brings me a message from Lieutenant Oka, who would like to talk to me about something, so I go straight over to see him. Despite the heat, the officer is wearing a new tunic over his shirt, and a pair of boots that shine in the sunlight.

He greets me with a smile.

'I have good news for you. The man you saw hanging in the courtyard cracked. In our last raid we caught a fifteen-year-old boy and his interrogation will take place this evening. Would you like to attend?'

The word 'interrogation' makes me feel sick. I compliment him on the competence of the Chinese interpreter and explain that my presence would be pointless. Quite unperturbed, he looks me in the eye and insists, 'You really don't want to come? What a shame. He's a very good-looking boy and I've already chosen several good strong men who'll keep him talking all night. It's going to be marvellous.'

It is thirty-five degrees in the shade, but the Lieutenant's words make me shiver. My only reply is to mumble something about not liking that sort of spectacle.

'I thought you liked that sort of thing,' he says, amazed.

'Lieutenant, your job is difficult and very important to the expansion of Japan and the glory of the Emperor. I wouldn't want to distract you from it. Allow me to decline your thoughtful invitation.'

I can see the disappointment flit across the man's face and he looks at me sadly. Lieutenant Oka has shaved so closely that the little moustache on his upper lip looks as if it is quite separate and might fly off at any moment.

'Come on, Lieutenant,' I say, patting his shoulder, 'you

get back to your work. The glory of the Empire depends on it.'

57

I HAVE waited for Min at the crossroads for a whole week, and in the afternoons I have gone up and down the boulevard outside the university in the vain hope of spotting his familiar face.

I find the address that Tang gave me; it is a run-down house in the poor, working people's quarter. There are children running in the streets shouting to each other and an old woman wearily beating out her sheets.

A neighbour appears.

'I have a book to give back to Tang.'

'She's been arrested.'

Fear is out stalking the streets of my town. The Japanese are determined to incarcerate anyone who opposes their rule. I am amazed that I am still free, and I lie awake at night listening for the soldiers' rhythmic marching, dogs barking and the muted sound of a fist knocking on our door. The silence is more terrifying than any amount of noise would be. I look at the ceiling, the dressing table with its mirror edged in blue silk, the writing desk where a vase of roses stands out against the darkness . . . All of these might be broken, ripped apart, burned. Our house would be like Jing's, just a charred skeleton.

I remember Min as he looked in the street. He had been running, his hair was a mess, he didn't know that prison was waiting for him just around the corner. He said, 'Jing loves you, he's just told me . . . you'll have to choose between us.' I was annoyed – it sounded like an insult, an order, and it wounded my pride. All I said was 'Don't let's make such a scene': those were almost my last words to him.

I miss Jing just as much as Min; his bad moods and his stiff attitude seem so endearing now. How can I save them? How can I contact the Resistance? How can I visit them in prison? To add to their miseries, they were born rich: the difference between their own bedrooms and the damp cells must be unbearable. They are bound to get ill. Apparently you can soften up the guards with money . . . I'll give everything I have.

A few shots ring out in the street and a dog howls, then the town drops back into silence like a pebble thrown into a bottomless well.

I am hot and I am cold. I am frightened, but my hate gives me strength. I open a drawer in the chest of drawers and find a little sewing case, a present for my sixteenth birthday. I take out the scissors with their gold handles and sharp, pointed little blades.

Pressed against my face, the precious weapon feels colder than a stalactite.

And I wait.

58

IN uniform and in civilian clothes, I am two different people. The first dominates the town with all the pride of a conqueror, the second is conquered by its beauty.

This Chinese man here is me ... I am amazed to see him taking on the accent, changing the way he looks and inventing an image for himself. When I put on my disguise I lose my normal points of reference, I am distanced from myself. It has almost made a free man of me, a man who knows nothing of my commitment to the army.

As a child I would often have the same dream: dressed as a black Ninja,[1] I would creep over the roofs of a sleeping town. The night was at my feet, and the occasional lights that twinkled were like the beacons on distant ships on a dark ocean. The town was not Tokyo, it was a place I did not know, and that made it all the more frighteningly exciting. In a narrow deserted street there were lanterns hanging under the eaves, swinging

1 The Ninjas were a troop of men specially trained for spying and assassinations who, according to legend, were first established at the end of the Heian era in the mountains around Kyoto.

their menacing glow in the wind. I would step softly from one tile to the next, right up to the edge of the roof, then I would leap into the abyss.

I resent Captain Nakamura for making me do this dirty work. I lack the intuition, the cynicism or the paranoia to be a spy and I certainly lack that professional eye which can pick out a darker mark on a dark piece of paper. On the other hand, I feel as if I am being spied on myself. Despite the stifling June heat, I wear a thick linen tunic so that I can hide a pistol in my belt, and when I sit at the go-board I put my hands on my knees so that my right elbow covers the weapon, which obstructs the fall of the cloth.

When I raise my right hand to move one of the stones, I can feel the steel brushing against me. The weapon is my strength and my weakness: I can open fire on anything that comes my way, but I can just as easily be shot in the back by a member of the Chinese Resistance.

I learned the strict rules of the game of go in Japan, where I would play in silence in the benevolent calm of a natural setting. I would be physically relaxed and my inspiration would diffuse its energy through my body, the rhythm of my breathing would guide my thoughts, and my soul would tentatively grasp the universal duality of things.

There is nothing spiritual about the game I am playing today. The Manchurian summer is as harsh as its winter. Anyone who has not been burned and dazzled by its sun can never know the sheer power of this black land. After the merciless training sessions, which leave me dehydrated and physically exhausted, the time I spend playing go with the Chinese girl is like an escape to a land of demons. The June heat permeates my dilated blood vessels and sharpens my senses. The smallest detail gives me an erection: her naked arm, the crumpled hem of her dress, the way her buttocks sway under the silky fabric, a fly buzzing past.

It is torture trying to maintain my dignity in front of this opponent. Over the last week her tanned skin has taken on the smooth, dark texture of a grape. Her clothes are sleeveless and these Manchurian dresses are so close-fitting that they make the women more disquieting than if they were naked. Our heads almost touch as we lean over the board. Thanks to the strong will forged by years of military discipline, I struggle against my impulses and crucify myself by playing the game.

My posting to China has taught me what greatness and what misery a soldier can know: he moves from one place to the next simply following orders and not knowing where he is going or why. A pawn among many others. He lives and dies anonymously in the name of a greater victory. The game of go is changing me into a senior officer who uses his men coldly and calculatingly: the stones make their steady progress, many condemned to die for the sake of a wider strategy.

Their loss becomes confused with the deaths of my comrades.

59

HUONG SCHEMES and cajoles to get any news she can, but it is more devastating every day. When she tells me that Jing's father has asked the Japanese authorities for his son to be given the death penalty so as to make a public example of him . . . I loathe her.

I feel complete despair in the face of my parents' indifference. Moon Pearl thinks that I am in love and keeps trying to worm the facts out of me.

'Are you upset about something, my sister?' she asks in a sugary voice.

'Not at all, Moon Pearl. It's the heat, it's making me ill.'

I find the servant Wang Ma's monotonous lamentations maddening and in the end I burst out laughing. My parents stare at me; this scandal is beyond the scope of their understanding and they don't know how to go about punishing me. Wang Ma runs out of the room in tears, and Mother slaps me. It is the first time she has ever hit me, my cheek burns and my head buzzes. Mother brings her hand up in front of her face and trembles as she looks at it, before taking refuge in her bedroom. Father stamps his foot and then he too disappears.

On the Square of a Thousand Winds I can relax in front of this stranger. He is punctual, but never complains when I am late; he rarely speaks and his face never shows any feeling. He stands up to the sun, to the wind and to my provocations. This internal strength that he has must spare him from a good many forms of earthly suffering.

I am here to forget myself; no one talks of arrests here, or of the Japanese occupation. News of the outside world doesn't reach us . . . only, the pain somehow manages to catch me out: a bird, a butterfly, a passer-by, a simple gesture – everything brings me back to Min and Jing. I get up and walk around the square.

The players are dotted about under the trees like earth statues scattered by Eternity. I am overwhelmed by a feeling of pointlessness. My legs feel shaky and my head spins. A grey curtain descends from the sky.

I stop the game.

My opponent looks up and peers at me from behind his glasses. He doesn't say anything, doesn't get angry. He plays without asking any questions. When I leave he watches me go until I am out of sight. My problems seem to have acquired a poetic grandeur; I have become a tragic actor and my only audience is this stranger.

60

THE SQUARE of a Thousand Winds has imprinted its smells on me and I now know its every tree, each chequered table-top, each ray of light.

There are old men, hard-bitten enthusiasts, who spend all day here with a fan in one hand, a teapot in the other and their birdcage hanging from a tree. They arrive at dawn and leave in the middle of the afternoon. When their two pots of stones stand open, it means that they are expecting someone; if they are closed, then they are waiting for someone to challenge them.

I was afraid that with time they would be able to tell a false Chinese man from the real thing, but I have swept aside this fear. Speech loses all its importance here and hands over its authority to the quiet clatter of the stones.

A false identity has been invented for me, but I have never had to use it. The girl has not even asked my name, an insignificant detail in a game of go.

Probably thinking that the fish has already taken the bait, she no longer makes any effort to charm me. She now seems to be saving her smiles and mischievous comments for the next player she manages to ensnare.

I do not know why, but she seems to be sulking with me. She has given up any form of greeting for a quick nod of the head, and she only emerges from her silence at the end of the session when we arrange our next meeting.

In the first few days I saw something of Sunlight in her, but now there is nothing about her, either from a distance or close up, that reminds me of the sophisticated and refined geisha. She moves despondently, her hair is messily plaited and there are black crescents at the ends of her nails. This sloppiness betrays her complete disdain for me. Acne spots have appeared on her forehead, and her face has lost all the simple grace that first attracted me. The whites of her eyes have lost their beautiful bluish gleam and her expression has darkened. Her lips are peeling and her hollowed cheeks make her look like a hardened soldier. The Chinese girl is changing into a man!

I overcome my disappointment by triumphing in the first direct conflict. The whites are surrounded in a tightening grip in the southern corner of the board and are gradually surrendering.

Apparently indifferent to this loss, she makes a note of our positions and hurries away.

61

'I MIGHT be pregnant,' my sister whispers.

After supper she follows me to my bedroom and I feel I have to congratulate her. I ask her when she saw the doctor.

She hesitates for a moment and blushes as she admits, 'I haven't been to see a doctor yet. I'm afraid . . .'

'Well, how do you know then?'

'My period is ten days late.'

My heart leaps. My period is ten days late, too.

'Are you sure?'

Moon Pearl takes my hands in hers.

'Listen, I'm normally very regular. This time it's for real! When I go to bed in the evenings I feel dizzy. In the morning I feel sick. All I want is pickled vegetables. They say that if you want to eat acid foods you'll have a boy. Do you think I'll have a boy?'

I am unmoved by my sister's happiness and I tell her she should talk to a doctor.

'I'm frightened. I'm terrified they might tell me I'm not pregnant. I haven't told anyone about this. It's a secret I can only share with you. Oh, my sister, I've discovered what it is to be happy again this morning! I put my hands over my belly and I could already sense the baby feeding on me inside. With him to give me strength, I can confront the infidelity, the abandonment and the lies. With him I can start a new life!'

I find my sister's exuberance chilling. She may long ardently for a child, but for me being pregnant would mean death.

After Moon Pearl has left, I sit down at my calligraphy table. With a fine paintbrush I sweep black strokes on the rice paper, counting the days since my last period over and over again. I should have had my period exactly nine days ago.

I flop down onto my bed, my head buzzing. I don't know how long I lie there feeling like that, but when I come round the clock is striking midnight. I get undressed and go to bed, but I can't get to sleep as I lie there in the dark. It is so strange to know that a new life is germinating inside another, that my body will produce fruit!

It will inherit Min's slanting eyes. If it is a boy, he will be happy and full of seductive charm like him, and wise and serious like my father. If it is a girl, she will have my red lips and my soft skin, she will be demanding and jealous like my sister, and she will have my mother's majestic bearing. Jing will take him or her for walks, proud but still bitter. On the Square of a Thousand Winds it will learn to play go and will eventually be able to beat me.

I stroke my stomach and come back to face reality: Min is a prisoner of the Japanese; when will he be released? I don't know his family. If I go to his house, they will drive me away. At school my name will be written up in shame, and I will be banned for ruining its reputation. The whole town will know about the scandal. Even if I accept the humiliation, my parents couldn't bear the sneering looks, the comments and the whispering. Children would throw stones at Moon Pearl in the street, jeering, 'Your sister is a whore!'

I switch the light on. My stomach looks flat, below my navel a line of fine fluffy hair runs down to the denser growth below. When our nurse washed me as a child, this hair used to make her laugh: she said it meant I would have a boy.

I will go down on my knees to my parents, I will beat my head on the ground to beg for their clemency. I will go and live at the ends of the earth and I will have my child there while I wait for Min and Jing to be freed.

That happy day will come: two men making their way towards a little cottage lost in the open countryside. The door opens . . .

62

ON 7TH July, our regiment – which has been posted to Feng Tai – loses a soldier after a night exercise. The Chinese army refuses to give us permission to search the town of Wang Ping. The two forces have their first exchange of fire.

On 8th July, a second confrontation flares up around the bridge of the Valley of Reeds.

On 9th July, the senior officers give the order to the various regiments garrisoned on the plain around Peking to prepare for combat. In Tokyo, the government, responding to international pressure, opts for a low profile: 'We should not aggravate the situation. The problem should be solved on the ground.'

The senior officers propose a ceasefire on four conditions: that the Chinese withdraw their garrison from the bridge in the Valley of Reeds; that they guarantee the safety of our men; that they hand over the terrorists; and that they apologise.

The Chinese reject the offer in its entirety.

On 10th July, Chiang Kai-shek's battalions move

towards Peking. The first reinforcements of our Manchurian regiments cross the Great Wall.

On 11th July, the Tokyo government finally acknowledges how urgent the situation is. It decides to send our battalions from Korea as reinforcements.

The earth underfoot shakes with the humming in the skies as the first bomber squadrons head for the Chinese interior. We feel a surge of pride as we see our flag painted on the fuselage: a crimson sun against immaculate white snow.

The men begin to shout, 'To Peking! To Peking!'

63

THE JAPANESE propaganda machine has been set in motion. The incident in the Valley of Reeds is already in the newspapers: their leading articles pillory the Chinese generals who publicly support the terrorist movement, violating the peace agreement. They are held wholly responsible for this latest crisis and must offer their apologies to the Emperor of Japan.

Mother, accustomed since her childhood to endless military conflicts, places her faith in prevailing apathy and in American diplomacy, which between them will calm the warmongers. Father sighs: once again the Japanese will improve their financial reputation. Public opinion is happy and confident: the Manchurian Emperor is keeping his country out of the conflict. For these cowardly individuals, the Sino-Japanese war will only ever be a fire burning on the opposite bank – a side-show.

White has become black, patriots are imprisoned alongside rapists and assassins, the foreign army marches through our streets and we thank them for keeping the peace. Could it be this disorder in the outside world that has turned my own life upside down?

My sister blossoms more each day, and there is no longer any sign of sadness on her face. She comes to see us wearing dresses that have been retailored to hug her slender body. Mother has heard the good news, and she is chivvying Wang Ma to make up the baby's layette.

I am dazed by how beautiful my sister is – each of her smiles weighs on my heart. Her son will be the joy of the whole household. Who cares if mine will be cursed.

In six nights Wang Ma has made a quilt for my future nephew. On a background of deep-red silk she has used tiny stitches to embroider lotuses, cherry trees, peach trees and peonies blooming in a celestial garden with swathes of green foliage and silvery mist. I smile as I look at this beautiful creation – my son will be wrapped in an old cloth, but he will be the most beautiful baby in the world.

64

COMING TOWARDS me, a huge hat on her head and in a dress that shimmers with every nonchalant sway of her hips, is a woman. I do not even have time to wonder who she is before she sits down opposite me, quite out of breath.

The sun filters through the weave of the hat, laying a mysterious veil over her face. A fine vein crawls over her left temple and disappears into her hairline. There are tiny, tear-shaped moles dotted on her dark skin.

A sharp slapping sound – the girl has just played her turn. Her hand stays on the board for a moment and I see that her nails are clean and painted orange.

I always listen to the sound the stones make, it betrays what the opponent is thinking. Early on in our game the Chinese girl would hold the stones between her first and second fingers and smack them gleefully onto the board; then, as the impact became quieter, it communicated her darker moods to me. Today it made a short, crystal-clear sound – she has rediscovered her confidence and vitality!

And she has actually undertaken a very original counter-attack.

While she walks through the woods, I think about the game in a very particular way: we have exchanged more than a hundred moves, but I forbid myself any calculations and I look at the board as a painter would an unfinished canvas. My stones are patches of ink with which I draw places and gaps. In the game of go, only aesthetic perfection leads to victory.

The Chinese girl comes back and when she sits down, her hat caresses my chest with its shadow. The ribbon around it flutters to the same accelerated rhythm as my heart. I cannot begin to imagine why she has dressed herself up as an adult. I do not know her name, how old she is, what her day-to-day life consists of. She is like a mountain that stands out clearly from a cloudy sky, only to melt all the more surely into the fog.

A humming sound interrupts my daydreaming. Our aeroplanes are flying overhead with bombs fixed below their steel wings. I watch my opponent out of the corner of my eye: she does not look up.

It is easier for my fellow officers to fly over China than for me to read the thoughts of the girl who plays go.

65

SOMEONE COMES into my room and shakes me violently. Is it Moon Pearl trying to wake me to go to the Sunday market? I turn my back on her, but instead of leaving she sits down on my bed, tugs my shoulder and starts to moan.

Irritated, I sit up abruptly, but when I open my eyes it is not my sister who I see but Huong, in tears.

'Come quickly! The Resistance fighters are going to be executed this morning.'

My words catch in my throat. 'Who ... who told you?'

'The matron in my dormitory. Apparently the procession is going to go past the North Gate. Get dressed! I think it might be too late.'

I put on the first dress I find, my fingers shaking so much that I can't button it up. I run out of the room still coiling my hair up into a chignon.

'Where are you going?' asks my father.

I find the strength to lie. 'I've got a game of go, I'm late!'

At the far end of the garden I bump into my sister as she comes in through the gate.

'Where are you going?' she asks, catching hold of my arm.

'Let me go. I'm not going to the market this morning.'

She gives Huong a hostile stare and takes me to one side.

'I've got to talk to you,' she says and it makes me shiver – does she know something about Min and Jing? 'I haven't slept all night . . .'

'Tell me what it is, please. I'm in a hurry!'

'I spoke to Doctor Zhang yesterday, I'm not pregnant. It's a false pregnancy,' she says, her eyes streaming with tears.

'You must go and see someone else,' I say to shake her off. 'Doctors can make mistakes.'

She looks up, her face distorted with anguish, and says, 'I got my period this morning.'

Moon Pearl throws herself into my arms and I drag her over to the house, where Wang Ma and the cook hurry to help me. I take advantage of the commotion to slip away.

There are hundreds of people thronging round the foot of the ramparts at the North Gate. The Japanese soldiers drive the crowd back by beating them with the butts of their rifles. My blood freezes in my veins as I come to terms with the fact that something terrible is going to happen before my very eyes.

An old man is jabbering away somewhere behind me: 'In the old days the condemned men would be blind drunk and they would sing at the top of their lungs before they died. Then the executioner's sabre would come down in a flash, and the body would often stay standing while the head rolled on the floor. The blood spurting out of the neck sometimes flew two metres into the air!'

The men listening to him click their tongues; these people are here because they view executions as a supreme form of entertainment. Furious, I step on the filthy old pig's foot and he gives a little cry of pain.

'They're coming! they're coming!' cries a child.

Standing on tiptoe, I can see a black ox pulling a cart bearing a cage with three men in it. Their mouths are full of blood and they are screaming out unintelligible sentences.

'They've had their tongues cut off,' I hear someone whisper.

I feel my heart constricting. Now that they have been almost tortured to death, all the condemned look the same: bloodied flesh still barely breathing.

The cart and others like it go slowly through the North Gate. Huong tells me she can't watch any more and will wait for me in town. But I am carried along by some indomitable inner strength and I want to watch them to the very end. I have to know whether Min and Jing are going to die.

The procession comes to a halt by a deserted stretch of wasteland. The soldiers open the cages and drive the prisoners on with their bayonets. One of them is nearly dead, and two soldiers drag him along like an empty sack of flour.

There are cries in the crowd. With the help of two sturdy servants, a finely dressed woman pushes past the people in her way, and reaches the military cordon.

'Min, my son!'

Far over there, a man turns round, falls to his knees

and kowtows three times in our direction. My heart stops. The soldiers throw themselves at him and beat him.

The condemned men kneel in a long line. One of the soldiers brandishes the flag and all the others raise their rifles.

Min's mother faints.

Min doesn't look at me, he doesn't look at anyone. Nothing exists except for the rustling of the grass, the quiet song of the insects and the breeze on the back of his neck.

Is he thinking about me – me carrying his issue inside me?

The soldiers load their rifles.

Min turns his head and stares hungrily at the person to his left. I eventually realise that it is Tang! They smile at each other. Min leans painfully towards her and manages to put his lips to the young girl's mouth.

The shots crackle loudly.

My ears buzz and I can smell rust mingled with sweat. Is that the smell of death? I sway as a profound feeling of disgust sweeps over me; my stomach contracts and I bend forward to vomit.

66

ORCHID, MY Manchurian prostitute, is slumped in her chair, sulking.

'You've changed,' she says.

I lie down on her bed, but instead of undressing me, as she usually does, she waves her handkerchief.

'You used to come and see me every two or three days, but you haven't been for almost two weeks. Have you met someone else?'

'I haven't seen anyone except you since I've been garrisoned here,' I try to reason. 'There are absolutely no grounds for you to be jealous.'

In fact her charms have had no effect on me for a while. I find her skin coarse, her flesh flaccid and our repeated couplings boring.

'I don't believe you,' she says, her eyes filling with tears. 'I love you and you love someone else.'

'You're being stupid. I could leave tomorrow and never set foot in this town again. I'll be killed one day. Why do you love me? You shouldn't get involved with someone like me who's just passing through. Love someone who can marry you. Forget about me.'

She cries all the more bitterly and I find her tears arousing. I push her onto the bed and take off her dress.

As she lies beneath me, Orchid's face begins to flush and she shudders and gasps between her sobs. I ejaculate, but the climax no longer has the intensity it once did.

Orchid lies next to me smoking and waving a fan with her free hand. I too light a cigarette.

'What are you thinking about?' she asks me gloomily.

I do not answer. The white cigarette smoke, dispersed by the wafting fan, rises slowly towards the ceiling in a series of scrolled waves.

'Is she Chinese or Japanese?' she insists.

I jump to my feet.

67

I WANDER aimlessly through the streets, my whole body stiff with horror.

'Go home,' says Huong.

'Leave me alone.'

'Please, go home.'

'I hate my home.'

'Well, cry then. Let it all out, please,' she begs me.

'I don't have any tears.'

She buys some stuffed rolls from a pedlar and says, 'Well, eat then!'

'They smell horrible.'

'What makes you say that? They smell good.'

'They're rotten. Can't you smell the vegetables are bitter? It's like blood. Oh, please throw them away or . . .' My stomach lurches and I am sick. Terrified, Huong throws the rolls to some cats stalking nearby.

I curl up on myself and hear Huong saying, 'Jing is alive.'

But this good news is not enough for me.

'I'm carrying a dead man's baby. I'll have to kill myself.'

'You've gone mad!' she says, shaking me by my shoulders. 'You're mad! Tell me you're delirious!'

I don't answer.

'Well then, hang yourself,' she says, hiding her face in her hands, 'no one can save you.' Then after a long silence she adds, 'Have you seen a doctor? It could be nothing.'

'I don't trust anyone,' I say.

'I'll find you a doctor.'

'What's the point? Min's betrayed me. I have to die.'

68

THE CHINESE girl arrived before me and she has put the stones out on the board. Her eyes are swollen and they have dark shadows under them; she has not combed her hair and it is rolled haphazardly into a simple chignon. She has slippers on her feet. She looks ill, as if she has just escaped from a hospital.

As I play she stares at the branches of a willow tree; the look in her eye is disturbing. Then she suddenly takes her handkerchief out and puts it over her mouth and nose as if she is feeling sick.

I am so obsessive about cleanliness that it tortures me to think that I smell and that this is what is distressing her. I breathe in deeply: the only smell I can distinguish is rotting grass, a warning that the rain is on its way.

Can she smell Orchid's perfume on me? The prostitute does use excessive amounts on herself and her clothes. She is possessive and jealous, trying to find a way of leaving her mark on me.

The sky has darkened and a clammy wind whisks up the leaves. The players tidy away their stones noisily, but the Chinese girl is lost in her thoughts and she does not move. When I point out that we are the only players left on the square, she says nothing but makes a note of our new positions on her sheet of paper, and leaves without saying goodbye.

Her strange behaviour arouses my suspicion and so I get up, hail a rickshaw and, hidden under its awning, tell the boy to follow her. She walks down the market streets, which are bustling with activity: traders taking down their stands, women bringing in their washing and pedestrians jostling past each other. Swallows under the canopies give out their little cries of distress. The sky is black, and fat raindrops begin to fall to the ground. Soon torrents of water are beating down on us, accompanied by thunderclaps.

The Chinese girl stops on the edge of a wood. I get out of the rickshaw and hide behind a tree as she dives into the green mist, her slender silhouette occasionally lit by the flashes of lightning. There is a silvery ribbon snaking through the branches, a river, swollen with rainwater, flowing east in a series of tiny whirlpools and brief sparkling reflections. On the horizon it becomes a wide expanse of black, which forges into the cleft of the sky.

The Chinese girl slips through the trees to the seething waters, and I launch myself after her. Then she stops suddenly and I have to grind to a halt and throw myself on the ground.

The young girl's stillness stands out starkly against the effervescent seething of the river. A succession of nearly a dozen thunderclaps rumble overhead. The trees bend in the fierce wind; a branch snaps and tears the trunk as it falls.

Scenes of the earthquake come back to me.

69

THE SMELL of blood has insinuated its way into my body, burrowing under my tongue and streaming out of my nose as I exhale. It follows me all the way to my own bedroom.

I wash myself in a basin of water, soaping my face, my neck and my hands, all impregnated with the fetid smell of death. Outside the rain falls. Why do the gods shed so many tears on our world? Are they weeping for me? Why don't these torrents from the skies wash away our suffering and our impurity?

I drop down onto my bed. The halting breath of the wind is like ghosts whispering as they rise up and recede. Could it be Min with Tang roaring with laughter?

Was he shut in the same cell as her? Did they hold hands as they watched their lives flowing like a river into the depths of the abyss? Had they kissed before I met Min? Had they made love? When she was free she probably wouldn't have given herself to him, but on their last night didn't they couple as the guard looked on, cheek to cheek, forehead to forehead, wound to wound?

She took him into her belly and into her soul. He

penetrated her on his knees, in penitence, he held her to him with all his might . . . his seed flowed, their blood mingled. She gave herself to him and he gave her deliverance.

I jump to my feet.

Min betrayed me, I must kill myself.

70

THE CHINESE girl turns round.

She looks like a ghost as she walks away from the river and out of the woods. All the streets look the same under the driving rain and they are all deserted; still the girl walks on – sometimes steady and upright, sometimes small and hunched – drawing me towards another world.

Suddenly she disappears and I rush backwards and forwards looking for her . . . in vain.

A rickshaw emerges from the mist and agrees to take me to the Chidori restaurant. Captain Nakamura is waiting for me in a private room, and he suggests we drink a toast to our glorious Emperor. After three glasses of *sake* and a few mouthfuls of raw fish, I stand up and bow deeply before announcing, 'Captain, I have failed in the mission you have entrusted to me. May I ask that you punish me severely for this failure.'

A smile plays on the corners of his mouth.

'Captain,' I go on, 'I am quite incapable of telling the difference between a spy and a peaceful citizen. I sit about on the Square of a Thousand Winds, forgetting my duties and playing go!'

He empties his glass of *sake*. He looks me in the eye and says very slowly and deliberately, 'Zhuang Zi[1] says, "When you lose a horse, you never know whether it is a good thing or a bad thing." An intelligent man never wastes his time.' Then he pauses briefly before adding, 'Did you know, Lieutenant, I was once in love with a Chinese girl?'

I flush, wondering why he has made this strange confession.

'I came to China fifteen years ago, to Tian Jing, where I was taken on to work in a Japanese restaurant run by a couple from Kobe. I did the washing-up, the cleaning, a bit of waiting at tables, and I was given bed and board in a tiny room. In what little spare time I had, I would sit at the window. On the other side of the street there was a Chinese restaurant famous for its stuffed dumplings. A young girl used to go in at dawn carrying provisions and she came back out late in the evening, carrying the dustbins. I was short-sighted and I could only just make out her slim shape and the long plait down her back. She wore red – it was like watching a walking pillar of fire. When she stopped I always felt she turned to look up at me, and through the haze I thought I could make out a smile – which made my heart beat faster.'

The Captain stops to refill my glass and drinks his own down in one. His face is getting steadily redder.

'One day,' he carries on, 'I found the courage to go into the restaurant pretending that I wanted to order one of their specialities. She was behind the counter and as I walked towards her I discovered her face, slowly, one feature at a time. She had thick eyebrows and black eyes.

1 Chinese philosopher (360? BC–280? BC), the founder of Taoist thinking.

I asked her for some stuffed dumplings but, as she didn't understand Japanese, I had to draw them on a piece of paper. She leaned over my shoulder to look and her plait slipped forward, brushing past my cheek.'

Another bottle is brought to the table, it is the fifth one that we have opened between us. The wind has dropped outside and the thunder has fallen silent, but we can still hear the regular patter of the rain.

'She couldn't even write her own name in Chinese,' he continued. 'We had no means of communication, but we spent our days catching each other's eye across the road, which seemed so wide to us, and we never tired of it. I could only make out the red of her clothes and the black of her plait, I had to reconstruct her face for myself even though I had only glimpsed it. I was poor and the only gifts I could offer her were little bunches of wild flowers picked along the edge of the road, which I threw under the window of her restaurant. In the evening she would give me stuffed dumplings fresh from the oven. I couldn't bring myself to bite into these delicacies crafted by her hands, so I would keep them until they rotted.

'One day it rained all afternoon, like today. Lots of customers had taken refuge in the restaurant, to eat warm noddles. It was after midnight when I got outside, and someone threw their arms round my neck – it was her. Goodness knows how long the Chinese girl had been waiting for me in that dark corner; her face was frozen, so were her lips. She was shivering from head to foot and, because of the rain, I couldn't tell whether she was laughing or crying. Weighed down by her, I leaned against the wall. As we kissed we whispered words of love to each other, each in our own language, and the rain drowned out what we were saying. I forgot the cold, the dark and the weather.'

The Captain sinks into a long silence, then looks up angrily and asks for another bottle. His hand shakes as he fills our glasses, and the *sake* spills over his clothes, but he doesn't notice. I can feel the blood hammering in my temples; I am following the Captain's story with all the unbridled fascination of a drunkard. He is struggling to speak . . . What terrible tragedy struck this man who now lives alone?

'The next day I went to a Japanese shop with all of my savings in my pocket. I didn't have enough money to buy a kimono – a beautiful *obi*[1] had to do. Without realising it, I was pouring poison onto our love with this present. Our relationship was soon discovered and a month later the Chinese girl disappeared without a trace.'

A painful silence weighs down on our table.

'Later, after I joined the army, I found out what had happened to her. The restaurant had closed years before and the owners, who turned out to be Chinese spies, had disappeared into thin air. When they'd found out that their servant was involved with a Japanese man, they'd condemned her to death . . .

'The moon is no more
The spring is no more
The spring it once was!
Only I, I alone
Am what I once was!'[2]

he recites. And then he weeps.

1 A wide belt used by the Japanese to secure a kimono.
2 Taken from *Ise Monogatari* about the Japanese province Ise in the eleventh century.

Tomorrow we will be nothing but earth and dust.
Who will remember the love a soldier once knew?

71

A FTER CLASS Huong drags me over to a quiet corner. 'I've found you a doctor,' she says, 'come with me.'

'Who is it? How did you find him?'

She looks round but the room is empty, we are the last to leave, so she whispers in my ear, 'Do you remember the matron in my dormitory who let me slip over the wall? Yesterday I told her that I was pregnant and looking for a doctor.'

'You're mad! If she starts gossiping, you'll be expelled and your father will make you shave your head and he'll send you away to the temple!'

'Don't worry, because I also told her that if she talked I would report her to the police for living off immoral earnings. I would tell the police that, to get money from the girls at school, she drove them into prostitution. Not only would she lose her job, but she would be condemned to a public hanging. I gave the old bat such a fright that she didn't waste any time finding me the discreetest of doctors.'

I follow Huong up to her dormitory, where she makes me dress as she thinks a woman of thirty would look.

The rickshaw goes through the flea market where the pavements are piled high with furniture, crockery, fabrics, knick-knacks, jewellery and scrolls of yellowed, mildewed, moth-eaten paintings. The people selling them are Manchurian aristocrats dressed in rags, who wander through the spoils of a bygone era hoping to trade in a jade snuffbox or an antique vase for an hour of escape in an opium house. There are just a few Japanese officers walking up and down, avidly examining their wares.

As a precaution, Huong asks the rickshaw to stop at the end of the street, and we walk down it for some 200 metres before climbing a crumbled flight of steps through a front door that leads us into a labyrinth of sheets, trousers and nappies drying on washing lines. The savage stench of urine and rotting eggs makes me bend right over to be sick.

At the far end of this corridor of washing we can see a row of rooms squashed under a heavily sloping roof. Each family has set up its cooking oven outside and there are clouds of flies spiralling around them.

'Hello-o,' Huong starts to call, 'Doctor Huang Pu.'

A dishevelled-looking woman appears on the doorstep and eyes us with contempt.

'Over there, at the end on the right,' she says.

On the door we find a sign written in faded ink: 'DOCTOR FAMED OVER THE FOUR SEAS FOR HIS HEAVENLY GIFT FOR BRINGING BACK THE SPRINGTIME OF YOUR LIFE. SPECIALIST IN CHANCRE, SYPHILIS AND GONORRHOEA.'

We knock at the door and a woman with permed hair

and a face devastated by make-up comes out, looks us up and down and then walks away, clicking her heels. Huong pushes me from behind and I stumble into a dark room. There is a girl lying huddled in a corner; she looks dead. Next to her there is a man smoking and he examines us closely.

'Which house?' he asks.

We take refuge in a corner of the room. The bitter smell of medicinal infusions and other indecipherable stenches suddenly hits me.

I don't know how long we wait before it is my turn to go into the doctor's consulting room. Doctor Huang Pu has white hair and there is so little of it that the Manchurian plait hanging down his back is as narrow as a pig's tail. He sits behind a black table, in front of an empty bookcase, stroking his little beard.

'Which house?' he asks.

'Liberal,' Huong answers for me.

'How old?'

'Twenty,' she says.

'What is the problem?'

'My friend's period is three weeks late.'

'Oh well,' he sighs. 'Open your mouth, stick out your tongue. Right, get undressed.'

I hesitate, and he says it again: 'Get undressed.'

Huong looks away. I hate myself and, with tears in my eyes, I start to unbutton my dress.

'Lie down over there,' he says, pointing to a board covered with a dirty sheet. 'Spread your legs.'

I think I am going to die. I clench my fists to stop myself crying. The old man comes over with a light in his hand. He looks, palpates, takes his time.

'Right,' he says, standing back up. 'No putrefaction. Get dressed.'

He asks me to put my right hand on the table, and he puts his first two fingers over my wrist. His yellow nails are more than five centimetres long and they curve at the end.

'The pulse is very irregular, I can sense your condition in it: you are pregnant.'

'Are you sure, Doctor?' I hear myself asking in a feeble whisper.

'Absolutely sure,' he says, taking the pulse on my left hand.

Huong gets to her feet behind me.

'You must have a remedy, Doctor?' she asks.

'Criminal, criminal,' says the old man, shaking his head.

Huong laughs nervously.

'Give us the prescription!' she says, throwing the huge golden bracelet that she wears round her wrist down onto the table. The old Manchurian thinks for a moment, eyeing the bracelet, then he picks up his calligraphy brush.

Huong sees me back home.

'Tomorrow, after lessons, I'll bring back the infusions and the whole thing can be forgotten,' she tells me.

'Don't go to so much trouble,' I say. 'The only way I can save my honour is to die. Look, take this jade bracelet. I don't want you to pay for me, I don't deserve it.'

But she puts it back on my arm.

'What use is something beautiful like that going to be to me? Tomorrow you'll drink your infusion and you'll be rid of this burden, but in a year's time I'll be married to a stranger and raped by him.'

72

THE DAY after the storm, a beautiful sky.

At this time of year there are jasmine sellers badgering everyone in the streets. I cannot resist their pleading and, thinking about the Chinese girl's tanned wrists, I buy a bracelet of the flowers.

When I see her on the Square of a Thousand Winds, I remember the strange figure she cut the day before as she stood by the river in the rain. What was she doing there? What was she thinking? Yesterday she wandered through the town like a madwoman with slippers on her feet, but today her hair is swept off her forehead and smoothed into a heavy plait, and she is playing coldly and shrewdly again.

Something about her has changed in the last twenty-four hours. Or am I no longer looking at her in the same way? Beneath her drab-coloured dress her breasts have swollen, her body has shaken off its childish stiffness and is now vigorous and supple. Despite her frown and the hard look in her eye, her gentle pink mouth cannot help but be attractive. There is a gloominess about her and she toys nervously with the end of her plait; as though it pains her somehow that she is blossoming with new life.

She moves a piece.

'Well played!' cries a man moving over towards our table.

On the Square of a Thousand Winds there are always people passing by, stopping to look and occasionally taking the liberty of giving advice. This man is barely twenty years old, with oiled hair and wearing far too much perfume – he annoys me.

I make my move.

'What a mistake! You should have put it there!' cries the young know-all, pointing to the board with his fine, pink hand with its white jade ring. Then he turns to the Chinese girl and says, 'I am a friend of Lu's. I'm from the New Capital.'

She looks up and, after a brief, polite exchange, she leads him away from the go-table.

The wind carries their voices over to me: an easy familiarity has been established between them and they are already using the informal form of address with each other. The Chinese language has five different tonalities; it is like music, but their conversation is one opera that I find unbearable. Piqued, I put my hand into my pocket and crush the jasmine flowers.

Since I have been coming to the Square of a Thousand Winds the game of go has made me forget that I am Japanese. I thought I was one of them, but now I have been forced to remember that the Chinese are another race, from another world. We are separated by a thousand years of history.

In 1880 my grandfather took part in Emperor Meiji's reforms while their ancestors were serving Ci Xi, the

Dowager Empress. In 1600 mine had lost in battle and were slashing their own bellies open, while theirs took power in Peking. In the Middle Ages, when the women in my family wore kimonos with long trains, shaved their eyebrows and dyed their teeth black, their mothers and sisters were piling their hair into buns on top of their heads. They were already binding their feet. A Chinese man and a Chinese girl understand each other before they even open their mouths. They are both bearers of the same culture, they are drawn to each other like magnets. How could a Japanese man and a Chinese girl ever love each other? They have nothing in common.

The girl stays away a long time. As it mingles and disappears among the trees, her green dress – which just moments ago seemed to express her desolation – suddenly seems to exude her freshness. Is that the image of China, the object of my passion and my hatred? When I am close to her, I am disappointed by her misery, but when she is further away I am obsessed by her charms.

She does not once look in my direction. I get up and leave.

73

CHEN TELLS me that Cousin Lu is now teaching go in Peking.

'And he's married, too,' he says, watching my reaction, but the news leaves me cold.

Chen lives in the New Capital and claims to be my cousin's best friend. He says that he presented Lu to the Emperor. To hear him you would think he was the most powerful man in Manchuria.

He is a Minister's son and seems so pleased with himself and happy with his life – I envy him his carefree existence. The past comes back to me in little snatches; it feels as if it was a hundred years ago: life was sweet. We were like him, my cousin and I: we thought we were the best players in the world. It was before my sister was married and we were both virgins; she would come and interrupt our games of go by bringing us tea and little cakes. The twilight would take its time, slowly weaving its crimson net across the sky. I hadn't learned about betrayal.

Chen returns that day to the New Capital. He leaves me a perfumed card with Cousin Lu's new address on it, and promises that he will be back soon to challenge me to a game of go.

I go back to my chair, but the table is deserted, my opponent has gone without leaving a note. I am so exhausted that I don't even feel angry. People come and go on this earth – each has his time.

I put the stones away as the sun lingers in the west and the clouds trail across the sky like long, cursive strokes. Who can decode these words that predict my fate?

I pick up one of the black stones, its shiny surface reflecting the sinking light. I envy its stony heart and icy purity.

Cousin Lu has fled from his disappointment into a new love, and I am glad that he has found happiness again so quickly. The Stranger has walked away from our game; for him, go is just a distraction. Men don't live for passion, they overcome periods of emotional turbulence quite comfortably and casually. Min proved that to me. The core of their lives is somewhere else altogether.

My rickshaw comes to an abrupt stop. There is a man bowing down to the ground in the middle of the road: it is the Stranger. He asks me to forgive him and begs me to carry on with our game the following afternoon. I nod vaguely at him and tell the rickshaw boy to carry on.

I have to leave him there, on his way.

74

'I N THIS world we walk upon the roof of hell and contemplate the flowers.'[1]

Only looking on beauty can turn a soldier's mind from his stubborn determination. But flowers care nothing for those who admire them; they flourish so briefly, only to die.

The latest dispatches have thrown the barracks into a state of excitement: having inflicted a series of defeats on the Chinese army, our divisions have advanced to the outskirts of Peking. Song Zheyuan and Zhang Zizhong's armies are now isolated and weakened, and they are more afraid of Chiang Kai-shek than of the Japanese. The generals fear that Chiang Kai-shek's troops will head north again to annex their territories, so they are refusing offers of Chinese reinforcements and suing for peace.

At the Chidori restaurant the anger builds from one table to the next. The most hawkish of the officers maintain that Peking should be conquered, while the more cautious are fearful that the Soviet Union will

1 From a poem by Issa, an eighteenth-century Japanese poet.

intervene, and recommend first and foremost that the Japanese presence in Manchuria be reinforced.

I did not go to see Orchid today so my body still feels fresh and supple, and I have not eaten much so I feel light and lucid. I do not allow myself to be dragged into the heated discussions, and I try in vain to stop my fellow officers from fighting.

The commotion goes on late into the evening and even back into some of their quarters. A few fanatical lieutenants open their shirts and swear that they will commit *seppuku* if the imperial army negotiates a peace with Peking, and this mention of blood fires the men up all the more.

I slip outside, and the wind blows the subtle scents of nocturnal flowers over my face as I cross the training ground. I am moved to think that I belong to a selfless generation, which aspires to a sublime cause. It is in us and through us that the spirit of the samurais — which has been stifled by all that is modern — is being reborn. We are living in a period of uncertainty, and the greatness that could be ours tomorrow makes the waiting all the more unbearable.

A mournful sound slices through the silence, the clear notes of a flute carrying on the air to me. I spotted a *shakuhachi* in Captain Nakamura's room. Could this be him in his melancholy, drunken state tormenting the instrument?

With each successive note the tune becomes lower until it is inaudible, then one strident note pierces the skies, cutting through me like a moonbeam projected onto a dark ocean. Today I am alive; tomorrow, at the front, I shall die. This fleeting moment of joy is more intense than an eternity of happiness.

The flute expires in an endless sigh and then falls silent. There are leaves flitting in the wind around me, and my eye is caught by a cicada clinging to a tree. Its armoured shell has split open, allowing the translucent body to emerge. The new life quivers throughout its length as it spreads, stretches, twists and sways. I wait for the moment when it breaks away from the husk, and I coax it to climb onto my finger. In the clear moonlight its soft, limp body looks as if it has been sculpted in jade by a skilled craftsman. Its wings spread along the silky skin like two drops of dew ready to fall. I touch the tip of its abdomen, but my finger barely comes into contact with it before its veins lose their coherence and its transparency is marred. The insect emits an inky liquid, its body slumps, and one of its wings swells and bursts, splattering black tears.

I think of the Chinese girl and of China . . . which we will have to crush.

75

'HERE'S THE infusion,' says Huong, taking a bundle of thick fabric from the bottom of her bag and unwrapping it to reveal a teapot. 'I've also brought you some cotton cloth. Apparently it makes you bleed quite a lot. Hide all of this. Does it smell strong?' she asks. 'I had to threaten suicide to get the matron to agree to boil up the ingredients at home. Take it before you go to bed, then lie down and wait. You should really drink it hot, but it should work cold, too – only the taste's more bitter. I'd better go, otherwise your parents will get suspicious. Be brave! Tomorrow morning you'll have got rid of all your bad luck.'

Mother leaves us before supper: she is going to sit through the night with my sister, who has been in bed for several days. I eat alone with Father and, as usual, his voice soothes me. I ask him about his translations and his eyes light up, he recites a few sonnets to me. I notice the silvery hair at his temples with a tinge of sadness. Why do parents grow old? Life is a castle of lies slowly dismantled by the passage of time. I regret not spending more time looking at the people I love.

Father asks me what I think of his poems.

'They're very beautiful, but I prefer our ancient verses, which say:

> When the flowers of spring fade,
> The autumn moon,
> So many memories come back to me![1]

'Or this one:

> What sorrow we know in this short life,
> Tomorrow I shall leave,
> With my scant hair in the wind,
> At the prow of a boat.'[2]

Father is angry, he can't bear my indifference to foreign civilisations. As far as he is concerned, it is this sort of cultural egocentricity that will be the downfall of China.

'I hate the English,' I explode. 'They fought us twice in order to sell us the opium that they had forbidden in their own country. I hate the French, who pillaged, destroyed and then burned the Spring Palace, the jewel of our civilisation. And ever since the Japanese have been laying down the law here in Manchuria, everyone cheers on the advances and the economic growth. I hate the Japanese! Tomorrow they will have invaded the whole continent, and then you'll be relieved because China will be annihilated and it will at last be forced to shake off its obscurantist attitudes.'

Hurt by what I have said, he gets to his feet, bids me good night and withdraws to his bedroom. I leave the

1 Poem by Li Yu, China, tenth century.
2 Poem by Li Po, China, eighth century.

dining room slowly and reluctantly: I was wrong to attack my father; his poetry is all he lives for.

I lock my door, draw the curtains and sit on the bed looking at the teapot in the middle of the table. I use scarves and handkerchiefs to make a strong rope. The grey smoke of the incense we use to daze mosquitoes rises slowly under my window.

Dying is so simple. A fleeting moment of suffering. In the blink of an eye you are over the threshold, into another world. No more pain, no more fears. You sleep so well there.

Dying is like rubbing snow together, setting fire to a whole winter of cold and ice.

I take up the rope and attach both ends to the posts on my canopied bed. The knot is firm and steadfast, like a tree that has been growing there for a thousand years. I sit back on my heels and look at it until my eyes hurt. I only have to get to my feet to stop my train of thought.

There isn't a sound. I lean forward to check that the knot is firm. I put my head through the loop, but the rope under my chin is uncomfortable. What I want is the emptiness, to be falling through the air. I am terrified by the dizzying pleasure of it: I am both here and over there; I am me and I am no longer me!

Am I already dead?

I take my head out of the noose and sit back down on the bed.

I get undressed, I am drenched with sweat. I dampen a towel in the basin and wash myself; the cool water makes me shiver. I pick up the teapot and drink the infusion, but it is so bitter that I have to stop several times to catch my breath. I put the sanitary pad stuffed with cotton between my legs, undo the knot, take apart the rope, and lie down on my bed with my hands on my stomach.

I wait, with the light on. Since Min's death I can't go to sleep in the dark. I am afraid of his ghost. I don't want to see it.

I dream of a forest where the dazzling sunlight filters through the trees, and a magnificent animal walks between them. It has a smooth golden coat, a mane like a lion's and the fine, slender body of a well-bred dog. I am furious that it has trespassed onto my property, and I call to a leopard, which leaps out from the trees and throws itself at the intruder. I suddenly become the injured animal, the leopard is tearing at my insides and ploughing through my entrails with its fangs.

I am woken by my own moaning. There is an unbearable pain running down from my swollen stomach and into my thighs, then it suddenly subsides. I get to my feet with some difficulty and head for the basin to cool my face in it. I drag myself to the kitchen, where it takes ten whole ladlefuls of water to appease my thirst.

Later my sleep is interrupted by the pain again. I fall off the bed, dragging the sheets and pillows with me. On the ground I cling to the table legs and struggle in vain against the intolerable cramps.

When the pain has abated, I bend over to see whether the blood has started flowing between my legs. The wodge of cloth is still spotless, and I think I can see Min mocking me in this stubborn whiteness. I can no longer feel the weight of my limbs. After the agony an obscure warmth runs from my toes all the way up my body, but instead of feeling pleasant, this comfort makes me shiver. I lie there, stretched out on the ground, looking at the mess in my room with perfect indifference.

A new spasm of pain, then another. The night seems so short, I am afraid it will come to an end and I will be found in this pitiful state. I should have killed myself.

The dawn has already tinged the curtains with white, and the chirping birds are announcing the new day. I can hear the cook sweeping the courtyard. Any minute now someone will find me, any minute now I will have to look into my father's eyes and I will die of shame.

I gather the last of my strength and get to my feet. My arms are shaking. If I tried to lift a feather, it would feel like a tonne.

I slowly tidy up my room as the morning sun blazes down on the floor tiles. My back is agony and, whether I stand up or lie down, I can't escape the feeling that I am going to give birth to a ball of lead. I sit down in front of the mirror, which shows me my devastated face. I put on some powder and a little make-up.

The blood comes as we are having breakfast, when I have stopped thinking about it, when my mind is completely empty. A scalding river coursing between my legs. I rush to the bathroom and find a frothy black liquid on the sanitary pad. I feel no joy and no sadness.

Nothing can make me feel anything any more.

It is time to go to school. To avoid the dishonour of staining my dress, I stuff the sanitary pad with everything I can find, cotton wool, fabric, paper. I put on two pairs of knickers, one on top of the other, and choose an old linen dress of my sister's, which I have always hated because it is such a drab colour and so shapeless. I do my hair in a single plait and tie it with a hankie.

When I get out of the rickshaw I walk slowly towards the school building, taking small steps. All around me there are girls running: in the morning the young are as

219

noisy as a flock of sparrows soaring up in the sky. One of my classmates taps me on the shoulder: 'Hey, you look like an old woman of thirty!'

76

I HAVE been waiting for the Chinese girl for an hour. When I was still a regular soldier, I loved being on guard duty. Standing with my gun clasped to my breast, I would spend the night listening out for the least sound. When it rained, I had a hood that cut me off from the outside world, and I became a foetus huddled in its own thoughts. When it snowed, the soft, fat snowflakes swirled down like thousands of syllables, white ink on black paper. As I stood there motionless with my eyes peeled, I felt as if I were turning into a bird or a tree; I was at one with nature in all its immutability.

The Chinese girl appears at last, sketching a smile by way of a greeting. I stand up and bow. She is slightly hunched, her eyelids look swollen and her face somehow crumpled as if she has just woken from a long, deep sleep. There are heavy lines at the corners of her mouth, and the hair that has strayed from her plait has been clawed behind her ears. She looks absent, dreamy, the way my mother used to look when she folded my kimonos.

She invites me to start. After the 200th move, the black and white stones now form a series of intertangled traps where those that lay siege are themselves besieged. We are battling for narrow corridors and cramped corners of territory. The Chinese girl replies to my move after a few minutes, her stone landing like a pin dropping in a silent room.

I am surprised at how little time she gives herself to think. I have such unpleasant memories of how on edge I was the last time we played that I have prepared myself to resist any form of external influence. I allow myself half an hour of meditation before I respond. Three minutes later the white stone has been played. Amazed by this brutality, I look up.

She quickly shifts her eyes and pretends to watch the other players over my shoulder. My heart beats faster, but I look down and try to concentrate. Incredibly, when I stare at the black and white pattern on the board I see the image of my own face!

I have hardly moved my black stone before her white one takes over a neighbouring intersection. She has never reacted so quickly and yet the move itself is irreproachable. I look up again, our eyes meet and she stares at me. A shiver runs through me and, to hide my uneasiness, I pretend to be thinking.

She carries on staring at me; I can feel my forehead burning under her gaze. Then suddenly her voice rings out: 'Would you do me a favour?'

'How could I be of use to you?'

'Let's leave this place, I'll explain.'

I help her make a note of our positions and put the stones away in their pots. When she has put everything away in her bag, she asks me to follow her. She walks ahead, and I follow behind. She takes small steps and a few strands of her hair beat the rhythm in the air as she walks on.

My heart feels heavy and a strange feeling of anguish comes over me. Where is she taking me? The trees part before her slender form and close in again behind me. The roads weave a vast labyrinth, and I am lost.

Sometimes she looks round and smiles; the coolness in her eye has gone. She lifts her arm to hail a rickshaw, and tells me to sit down next to her.

'The Hill of the Seven Ruins, please.'

The sunlight streaming through the blind throws a golden veil over her face. Tiny motes of dust fall twinkling from the ceiling and come to rest on the ends of her eyelashes. I try desperately to keep to the far end of the narrow bench seat, but even so when we come to a bend in the road my arm brushes against hers. Her icy skin leaves its imprint on mine as if I have been bitten. She pretends not to notice. The distinctive fragrance of a young girl wafts from her neck, a blend of green tea and soap. The rickshaw trundles over a pebble and my thigh presses against hers.

I am strangled by my feelings of arousal and shame.

I want to hold her so much it is killing me! Since I cannot put my arm around her shoulders and rest her head on my chest, I would be content just to brush my hand over her fingers. I watch her face carefully out of the corner of my eye, ready to abandon myself like a moth drawn to a light. But the Chinese girl's face remains closed. She sits there with her brows knotted, watching the rickshaw boy's back as he runs.

I keep my hands clamped on my knees.

The rickshaw stops and we get out. I throw my head back and my eyes climb up a wooded hillside. At the top, lost in the sunlight, I can just make out a pagoda overlooking the exuberant vegetation.

In front of us a slate path snakes between shrubs and tall grasses, and disappears as it climbs upwards through the shade of the trees and the reeds.

77

IN CLASS Huong passes a note to me under the table. I unfold it and read: 'Well?'

I tear off a sheet and reply: '!'

A few minutes later another missive arrives, and the writing is so violent that it has broken through the paper in places: 'My father arrived this morning. He's taking me away with him at the end of the academic year. I've had it!'

Our lessons end this week. I despair at the thought of Huong being married off to the son of some minor country dignitary, and the effect of this emotion brings on the contractions again. As soon as the bell sounds, I bow to my teacher and hurtle to the toilets with my bag full of wadding.

Huong has followed me and is waiting for me outside the door. Her lips are trembling and she can hardly articulate. I drag her away from the other pupils and she bursts into tears. My stomach is hurting, but Huong throws herself in my arms so that I can't bend over to repress the spasms. I hold her to me and my sweat mingles with her tears.

She has to have lunch with her father, and she begs me to go with her. She wants to negotiate a year's reprieve.

With his silk tunic and his watch on the end of a gold chain, my poor friend's father is a farmer dressed up as a gentleman. He takes us to a luxurious restaurant and we have hardly sat down when he starts enumerating the expenses of her education, all that money earned by the sweat of his brow.

'Anyway,' he says, striking the table with his fist, 'all that nonsensical investment is coming to term. You're packing your bags.'

His yellow teeth are disgusting. Huong is white as snow, she daren't open her mouth.

I feel terrible. Every now and then the clatter of plates and the hubbub of conversation swell to a deafening thrum. I drop my chopsticks and bend over to pick them up. Huong leans over and whispers, 'Go on! Say something!'

What should I say? Where do I start? My friend is putting all the weight of her happiness on my shoulders. Struggling against the pain gnawing away at me, I drink three cups of tea in quick succession and, feeling a bit stronger, I try to explain to the old crook that his daughter really should finish her studies and get a diploma.

'How much does a diploma cost?' he splutters in my face. 'I can't read and I'm doing well enough! I've had enough of ploughing my money into this chamber pot. She needs to show me a bit of a return now! And as for you, Miss Stick-your-nose-in-everything, you should think of your own future. You're not bad-looking, your parents should hurry up and find you a good match.'

I stand up and leave the restaurant. Behind me I can hear the old boy shrieking with laughter.

'Is that your best friend? Little bitch. I'll tear your eyes out if you see her again. After lunch I'm taking you to buy some dresses. You'll see, you'll have the best dowry in the region.'

I hail a rickshaw out in the street.

There has been less blood since midday, but I am exhausted. I long to sink into a deep sleep. Mother is at home: to return now would mean being exposed to her sharp eye. If I go to bed it would be like admitting that I am ill, and they would soon find the cause.

I snooze in the rickshaw and, after making the boy wander aimlessly around for a long time, I remember I have arranged to play go. I return home immediately, but I stay hidden in the rickshaw and send the boy to ask the housekeeper to get the two pots of stones.

The terracotta statue is already there on the Square of a Thousand Winds.

Our game is moving towards its final phase, and I regain some of my old energy and dignity as I play. But time is against me: I am dazed by the sunlight while my opponent meditates at length. I close my eyes, but my ears are filled with endless waves of muffled rustling sounds. There is a huge clearing opening out at my feet, and I lie down on the cool grass.

I am woken by the click of a stone on the board: my opponent has just played his turn. Our eyes meet.

'Would you do me a favour?' I have hardly formulated this request in my mind before it leaves my mouth. He doesn't even know my name.

I get up, feeling feverish and racked by the pain in my stomach. I need to run away from these players, from the game of go, from the whole town.

I get into a rickshaw and my opponent sits down next to me. He has more pronounced muscles and wider shoulders than Min; as a result, the bench seat seems narrow. Lulled by the rolling motion, I feel as if I am setting off on a long journey. I am no longer myself, I am floating.

The rickshaw stops at the foot of the hill, and I start to climb. The Stranger follows me, still silent, as the wind wafts the bitter perfume of wild flowers over us. My legs are shaking and I can't breathe very easily, but luckily I have started to sweat and the fever seems to be subsiding. I wait for the Stranger, who is walking slowly with his hands crossed behind his back. He looks up, but lowers his eyes at once.

Who is he? Where is he from? Do I really need to ask these questions? The answers would only erase the peculiar and familiar, disturbing and fleeting figures which people our dreams.

We go past the path that leads to the place where I sat on the chipped marble carved into the shape of a flower and faced Min, waiting for my first kisses.

After the broken-down pavilion, I head deep into a pine wood where the path peters out. There are insects calling, the shiver of wind has dropped and here and there rays of sunlight stream through like waterfalls. A clearing.

Love has been buried for ever under the leaves at my feet.

I lie down on the ground and rest my head on my bag.

The grass tickles my arms where I bend the stalks under my neck.

I want to sleep.

78

S HE LEANS towards me in the middle of the clearing. 'Watch over me. Don't wake me if I go to sleep.' And she lies down in the grass under a tree, with her head resting on her school bag.

I am so amazed I do not know what to do. I understand everything and I understand nothing. She wants me with her under this tree. This girl, who understands how dangerous it is to be surrounded, who calculates ten moves in advance to avoid a trap ... has just stepped into the web of human emotions and handed herself over to me.

I touch the gun hidden under my tunic. Could she have discovered my true identity? Is she setting a trap for me? The trees and bushes form a threatening circle around me. I listen intently: nothing except for birdsong, the monotonous chirping of the cicadas and the whisper of a spring.

I go over to the Chinese girl. She has curled up on her left side with her eyes closed and her legs slightly bent. I wave a fan over her to drive away a bee, which has mistaken the fine down on her face for the pistil of a flower. She does not react; I lean closer. Her chest rises and falls with the regular rhythm of her breathing. She has gone to sleep!

I sit down against the tree that casts its shade over us. There is something touching about the young girl's deep sleep. I decide to wait until she wakes, and surrender to the soothing peacefulness of drowsing, sheltered from the heat. My eyelids grow heavy and, lulled by the insects' monotonous humming, I close my eyes.

How did this story start? I lived in Japan and she in Manchuria. One snowy morning our division set off for the mainland. From the bridge we could see a misty sea, constantly troubled by the buffeting waves. China was a distant, invisible land; it was still an abstract idea to me. From all this grey immobility, railways sprang up, and woods and rivers and towns. The tortuous path of fate took me to the Square of a Thousand Winds where this adolescent girl was waiting for me.

I do not remember my first game of go, for I learned to play more than fifteen years ago. Later I made a point of challenging those adults who condescended to grant me handicaps. They would make fun of my opening tactics; my sieges were as leaden as a full meal in a starving man's belly. At that stage in my life I could not imagine the future, no more than I could the past. The game of go has taken many years to initiate me into the freedom of slipping between yesterday, today and tomorrow. From one stone to the next, from black to white, the thousands of stones have ended up building a bridge far into the infinite expanse of China.

I open my eyes again. Up in the sky a mountain of clouds with deep valleys throws an eerie relief over the clearing. The grass, branches and flowers that were invisible in the incandescent light now have clear outlines as if newly chiselled and defined. The trees rustle in the wind, but the Chinese girl sleeps on through this concert of *kotos*, flutes and samisens. Her dress covers her down to the ankles. Dead leaves that have fallen onto her have transformed the violet-blue fabric, creased along the undulations of her body, into a sumptuous drape embellished with folds, furrows and unfurling waves. Will she get up and dance here on this stage, which is the preserve of the gods and of all those who dream?

The sun emerges from behind a cloud, throwing a mask of gold over the sleeping girl's face. She moans and rolls over onto her right side, her left cheek marked by twigs. I open out my fan silently and hold it over her head. Her knitted eyebrows relax and the hint of a smile appears on her lips.

I gently caress her body with this artificial shade. An uncontrollable surge of pleasure sweeps over me. I shut the fan abruptly.

How could I have confused modesty with indifference; how could I have been immune to her messages? She already loved me when I thought of her as a little girl. It must be the power of this passion that she has kept hidden for so long that has made a woman of her. Here, today, she is offering herself to me with extraordinary audacity. Compared to her I seem a coward, and only moments ago I was afraid this was a trap, I hesitated to take her in my arms, fearing for my own life.

The war is just about to explode. Tomorrow I will leave for the front and I will abandon her. How could I exploit her virginity with a clear conscience?

A soldier deserves death, not love.

I close my eyes and try to regain my lucidity. I set

against this sun-drenched clearing the image of a snowfield, trenches dug out of frozen earth, and decomposing bodies.

Something knocks against my leg: the Chinese girl is curling up more tightly. She looks as if she is in pain. Is she cold? It can only harm a cherished creature like her to sleep on the bare ground for too long. I shake her gently, but instead of waking up she shudders and goes on with her nightmare. I take her hands and hold them on my knees. She seems to calm down.

I think I can make out a glimmer of happiness through her closed eyelids.

79

I HAVE to go and see Moon Pearl on the other side of town. Mother holds me back, afraid that I won't be home in time for lunch. I laugh at her concern and say, 'Look!' as I stamp my foot and jump off the ground. Instead of falling back down, I rise up into the air, beating my wings. Our house is reduced to a brick, then a grain of sand lost in the garden of our town.

There is not one cloud, not a single bird in front of me. I glide and bank, carried by the wind, spiralling tirelessly upwards into infinity. Suddenly eternal night falls, a deep, cold darkness. The stars don't twinkle, they just stare thoughtfully. Drawn by their motionless brilliance, I prepare to fly up to them when a sharp pain pierces through my entrails.

I tumble back down, paralysed by the spasm and flapping my hands, my feet and my wings, but there is nothing to hold me, nothing to carry me. In the blink of an eye I travel back across my town, into my house, and continue to fall into the abyss.

My whole body is on fire. I feel sick. I scream in horror.

Someone grabs hold of my body as I fall. Who has arms long enough to fish me from the depths of the ocean? I stop moving. I mustn't move and then he will be able to extricate me from the darkness. Firmly but gently he leads me back out of the depths, towards life, like a midwife guiding the baby to its birth. The warmth from his palms is transmitted into my skin and spreads through me. I am naked, creased, red, huddled. I am intimidated by the light, by the rustlings of the world. I shudder with pleasure.

When I open my eyes I look straight into the eyes of a stranger, and leap to my feet in surprise. He stands up too, but I grab my bag and run away.

The sunset has thrown its crimson cloak over the hills. Yesterday I still couldn't look the flaming red of twilight in the eye; it reminded me of that red sun suspended in the mist on the morning of the execution. Now I look at it defiantly.

I take a long time to find a rickshaw. The sun is shrinking on the horizon, and crows launch themselves into the wan darkness. Soon I am swallowed up in the night. The road goes through a huge field of wheat where fireflies zigzag back and forth.

The moon looks like a line of chalk drawn on the sky.

The Stranger is following me, and I am both frightened and delighted by the sound of his footsteps. Will he catch up with me?

I am no longer frightened of ghosts: Min and Tang went back to their graves last night – may they rest in peace! I am a different woman now and I carry my name the way a cicada still carries with it the memory of the ground in which it slumbered before its metamorphosis. I am not afraid of anything any more. This life is just a game of go!

The man is keeping his distance.

A rickshaw goes past and I call it. I climb in alone and the boy starts to pull away.

'Wait!' The Stranger puts out his hand and holds back the rickshaw. 'Wait,' he says again in a trembling voice.

Standing alone under a street light, he looks disproportionately tall and alone. He seems to caress my face with his eyes.

I lower my gaze and stare at the rickshaw boy's back.

The rickshaw swings into motion, and the voice fades in the distance behind me.

'You will come and play tomorrow, won't you?'

I look up. There are tears sliding over my eyes, hurting me, and through their fog I look hungrily out onto the black countryside. I must dry these ridiculous tears. The shadows of passers-by stumble on the pavement, all the houses are lit up and hundreds of lives unreel through the windows.

80

I AM exhausted and decide to go to bed without any supper. There on my bed I find the mail that arrived during the afternoon.

With all the fluency and calm appropriate to an educated woman, Mother records the event of the month: Little Brother has set out for China.

'At first I was amazed by the silence in the house,' she writes. 'To stop myself thinking about the fact that we are all apart, I have busied myself tidying up. Organising things helps me forget that you're not here. When I came across the kimonos you wore as children, I couldn't believe you had grown up so quickly, that you were both already fighting for the Emperor.'

In his letter, Little Brother begs me to forgive him: he did not have time to ask my permission to leave our mother.

'We will see each other soon in China, at the front. You'll be proud of me at last!'

I sigh at his naivety, I would have liked him to have stayed where he was, protected from the cruelties of war. But how could I forbid him choosing his country before his own life? As a child he idolised me, but after Father's death he rebelled against my authority. Now I am his role model once again.

I feel sorry for my mother. Her men have left her and the gods have condemned her to living alone. I cannot imagine her suffering when she receives two urns containing her sons' ashes.

A game of cards is in full swing in the neighbouring room. I can hear the players shouting through the wall.

'I'll double my stake!'

'Me too!'

Every soldier has his own way of defying the future.

I think about my mother, her slender frame wrapped in a widow's kimono. Next to this heartbreaking image I see that of the Chinese girl curled up on the grass. Despite the difference in age and background, they have a common fate: the insurmountable sorrow of an impossible love.

Women are the offerings we make to this vast world.

81

MOTHER QUESTIONS me severely when I return home.

'Where were you? Why are you home so late?'

I lie badly, but for some strange reason she pretends to believe me. Father is reading the paper on the sofa, an enigmatic smile playing on his lips. He doesn't say a single word to me all evening.

I gobble down the left-overs in the kitchen – my appetite is back, and for two days now I have been more able to tolerate smells. Mother comes in silently and sits down facing me. In the half-light the red lacquered table looks almost black, polished so meticulously by the cook that it is as smooth as a mirror. Unable to avoid looking her in the eye, I count the grains of rice on the ends of my chopsticks.

Descended from a line of Chinese nobility whose women breastfed the Manchurian emperors, Mother has seen all their pomp and splendour eradicated, and her heart has been hardened. She seals her memories away in chests, and now she watches the world deteriorate with all the cold dignity of a wronged woman.

Her time in England put her off China. In fact my sister often used to say that, had it not been for Father's insistence, Mother would never have come back. Unlike the majority of Chinese women who overflow with maternal love, Mother maintains a courteous distance with us, which forbids any show of affection. When she is angry it is only ever over insignificant details: being a few minutes late, a lack of courtesy, a crumpled book . . .

'You've lost weight,' says Mother.

My heart sinks: what is she saying?

'You don't look well. Let me take your pulse.'

I slowly extend my left arm to her, and carry on eating with my right hand. Could she be about to discover my secret?

'Weak and irregular,' she says after squeezing my wrist for a while. 'I must take you to see my doctor. I'm worried about your health. Young girls your age are weakened by the changes in their bodies. That's why the ancients used to marry them very young, to stabilise them.'

I don't dare argue with her.

'You must have some swallows' nest soup,' she says, getting up, 'it warms the blood and the intestines, it puts some harmony into the ebb and flow of energy. Tomorrow we will go and see old Master Liu. He can recommend some medicinal infusions. Then I'll take you to the American hospital. Western medicine fills the gaps in our own. The holidays start at the end of this week and you will stop playing go on the Square of a Thousand Winds. Your sister is coming home, and I'll keep both of you under my roof to get you both back to health.'

I have absolutely no desire to be examined and I tell her that I won't have time to go to the doctor tomorrow.

'You don't have lessons at the end of the afternoon,' she replies.

'I have to finish my game of go. It's very important.'

Mother is angry, but her voice stays calm.

'I have given you too much freedom, you and your sister. It does you no good. Cancel your game of go,' she says, heading for the kitchen, then she turns in the doorway and says, 'You're dressing very badly at the moment. That dress belongs to your sister, it's too long for you and the colour doesn't suit you. Where are the dresses I had made for you a couple of months ago?'

Back in my room, I slump down onto my bed. I lose less blood in the night, but I still sleep restlessly. Huong, dressed in red and covered in jewels and embroidery, bows to a horribly ugly man. She is in tears and she looks like a goddess who has been banished from the heavens and is purging her pain in squalor. A stranger notices how sad I am, and takes my hand. His hand is as rough as a pumice stone and it soothes my agitated nerves. Behind him I can see Min under a tree in front of the Temple of the White Horse. He smiles at me and disappears into the crowd.

When I wake up in the morning my whole body feels slack and my skin dry. To please my mother I put on a new dress and the stiff fabric chafes me.

At the temple crossroads I glance over to the tree where Min was standing in my dream. There is a man crouching there and when I meet his eye, my blood freezes: it's Jing!

I jump out of the rickshaw. He has lost ten kilos, his face is hidden under a hat and covered by a black beard, but I can see that it is distorted by scars. When I head over towards him, he backs away. For a long time he doesn't say anything, he just stares at the ants climbing up the tree in an unbroken line.

'I betrayed them,' he says in such a sullen voice it makes me shiver. 'Their bodies were thrown into a common grave. I couldn't even go and make my peace by their tombs. It seems only yesterday that Min was still here, so full of life, so happy.'

Jing bangs his head against the tree trunk. I take his arm, but he shakes me off.

'Don't touch me,' he says. 'I confessed everything, told them everything. It was as easy as pissing, I wasn't ashamed. I wasn't thinking about anyone. The words just came out, I couldn't stop them. It was intoxicating, destroying everything . . .'

Jing bursts out laughing, shaking his head vigorously.

'You're the only person who doesn't seem to look at me as if I were a monster,' he says. 'My father prays that I'll die and he's forbidden my mother to see me again. It's as if I'm wearing the mark of evil on my brow now.'

He thumps the tree so hard with his fist that his hand splits open.

I pass him a handkerchief and he whispers, 'I can't go back to the university now. I'm ashamed. I live like a rat, running away from my friends and frightening children in the street. I can't sleep at night. I'm waiting for the Resistance Movement to send out their killers. They'll drag me along the ground and point their guns at me, saying, "You betrayed our trust, you sold your dignity, and in the name of the Resistance, in the name of the Chinese people, in the names of the victims and their families, we send you on your way to hell . . ." You'll see my body in the street, right here in the middle of the crossroads, with a sign round my neck: "He betrayed, now he's paid!"'

I feel sorry for Jing, but I can't find the words to comfort him. He looks at me searchingly, then throws himself at me and squeezes my hands so tightly that it hurts.

'You should know the truth. Min was married to Tang in prison so that he could be united with her to face death. I've only ever loved you. Of the two of us, Min betrayed first: he betrayed you and that disgusted me. I refused to follow him for your sake. I wanted to marry you, I wanted to protect you, I wanted to see you before I died and to tell you how much I loved you. I traded dishonour for love. Say you understand! Say that you don't despise me!'

I suddenly feel terribly light-headed, and I try to free myself from Jing's embrace. He stares at me and says, 'I've got two passports for the inner territories. Come with me. We'll go to Peking, we can carry on with our studies there. I'll work to pay for food for you, to make you happy. I'll be a rickshaw boy if I have to. The train's at eight o'clock tomorrow morning. I've already got two tickets. Come with me!'

'Let me go!' I say, fighting him off.

'You hate me,' he says with a sigh. 'I was stupid to think that anyone could love someone as pathetic as I've become. Go on then, look after yourself and forget about me.'

He shrugs his shoulders, lowers his head and stoops despondently as he moves away with his hands in his pockets.

'Wait! I need to think,' I say. 'Let's meet here tomorrow.'

He turns back and looks at me in despair.

'Tomorrow or never!' he says, moving away, a bitter, downtrodden figure hugging the temple walls. I notice that he is limping and that he drags his left leg like a rotten branch. The sight of this hurts me, I lean my forehead against the tree and close my eyes. The bark communicates the feeble heat of the morning sun to me. It feels as if Min is there next to me.

'I hate you.'

He smiles and says nothing.

82

A WOMAN is bathing in thermal springs, her naked body glistening under the water where it writhes and twists like a slender leaf. Next to the pool there is a blue cotton kimono hanging on the branch of a tree, swaying delicately in the caressing breeze.

The strident wail of the bugle interrupts my dream, and I reach mechanically for the clothes folded on top of my shoes at the foot of the bed. I heave my pack onto my back and hurry outside.

As the troops gather, whistled instructions shriek from every direction. The regiment sets off, then the order comes from the head of the formation and we start to run. The barrack gates draw open and the guards salute us. Then the gates of the town open and the chill, gloomy air of the countryside whips my face.

I am dripping with sweat, but instead of diving into the woods as we have done on our previous exercises, we continue along the main road. I am choked with apprehension: we are heading for Peking.

When the sun appears on the horizon we are already far from the town. I struggle to put myself in a state of readiness, to see myself as a soldier fit for battle, and I call on death to give me strength. But, curiously, instead of appeasing me and filling me with strength as it always has before, this prayer makes me even more nervous.

The warm, easy months I have spent in the garrison evaporate in a flash. Did the town of A Thousand Winds really exist? And what about the girl who played go, was she just the heroine in some wonderful vision? Life is an infernal loop where the day before yesterday has merged with today, and yesterday has been jettisoned. We think we are moving forward in time, but we are always prisoners of the past. Leaving . . . that is a good thing: if I had stayed on the Square of a Thousand Winds I would have let myself be destroyed by the most tenacious of instincts: loving, living and bringing forth children.

I hear the whistle signal to halt the march, and our platoon bunches together like an accordion as we stop to catch our breath. I take my flask off my pack and pour the sun-warmed water down my throat.

A new order comes through: about turn, the back of the formation becomes the head of the column. We are going back to the town. Cries of joy go up among the men and, urged on by the officers, the soldiers set off again. I abandon myself, carried along on this wave of happiness.

83

IN CLASS Huong keeps scratching her desk agitatedly with her nails. I tear off a piece of paper and write her a note: 'Stop it! You're driving me mad with your scratching.'

'Please don't be hard on me,' she replies in careful writing, 'I didn't sleep at all last night.'

'Jing has asked me to go to Peking with him. Come with us! He'll get you a passport and a ticket, and we'll be free there!'

'You can never trust a coward,' she scrawls. 'You should pity him, but don't go with him.'

'Jing's not like the others.'

'Traitors are all the same. You be careful!'

'When you go back to the country with your father and you marry your stranger,' I write more slowly, 'you'll be betraying yourself, then you'll know how painful it is to be weak, to be a coward.'

'Leave me alone, I've made my choice. I'm not taking my chances with you in Peking. I don't want to run away from reality by running away from life itself. Stay here!'

she begs. 'War is going to break out here in China. No one's going to be able to escape from the horror.'

'You're talking like a married woman. Has your father brainwashed you?'

'I've been thinking. I want a man in my life. That's all I want.'

'You're different today, Huong, you're strange.'

'We've been corrupted by fiction,' she writes bitterly. 'Love and passion are just monstrous creations dreamed up by writers. Why would I dream of freedom if it weren't the way to love? Given that love doesn't exist, I've agreed to be made a prisoner of life. I want my suffering to be rewarded by the pleasures of clothes and jewellery and an easy sort of happiness.'

'Have you gone mad? Why are you coming out with all this rubbish?'

It's a long time before Huong replies, her pen scratching squeakily on the scrap of paper: 'I've never admitted this to you, but I met a banker two years ago and I became his mistress yesterday. He will come and pick me up from school later and he'll set me up in one of his houses. He will pay my father a substantial sum and I won't see the old man again.'

I wonder which of the two of us really is mad, but our heated correspondence is interrupted by the bell. I put my things away in my bag and leave the room without saying a word to Huong.

'You're ashamed of me, aren't you?' she says, stopping me in the street.

I shake my head and start to move away from her quickly. She throws herself after me.

'Please,' she begs, 'don't abandon me! Don't go to Peking! I can feel that something terrible will happen to you there. Swear to me that you won't see Jing again. Swear to me that you'll stay! I'll tell your parents. They'll shut you in . . .'

I barge past her and she trips and falls. I immediately regret knocking her down, but I can't find it in myself to hold my hand out to her, and I run away.

84

ORCHID IS surprised and obviously very happy to see me. In a split-second she has slipped out of her dress and taken off my uniform. I let myself be manipulated. Her nakedness gives me an erection and the pleasure I experience as I penetrate her is as chaotic as the half-day that has gone before. The Manchurian girl screams and her cries give me a headache. Then she suddenly loosens her grip and tries to push me away, but I do not break away from her until I have reached a violent climax. She writhes on the bed, hiding her crotch with her hands and sobbing. I cannot believe it. This mad woman is still jealous!

I gulp down a cup of tea and sit on a chair. As she is still snivelling, I wash myself meticulously and dress to leave.

'Go away!' she shrieks in a cracked voice. 'Go away, and don't come back again.'

I head for the door, but she throws herself at me, showering my boots with her tears.

'Forgive me,' she moans, 'don't leave me . . .'

I push her aside with my foot.

As I head for the Square of a Thousand Winds I realise that I am the most pitiful man in the world – something in me has broken. I have the same feeling that I had as a child after the earthquake: an empty, inescapable feeling and a constant buzzing in my ears. Reason tells me I should not go back to the go-table, but my legs keep carrying me there. I want to run away from what I am losing, but instead I run headlong towards disaster.

The Chinese girl is already there, wearing a new dress. Her stiff collar, held tightly closed by two self-covered buttons, gives her face a tragic sort of dignity. My heart is beating painfully fast and my face is burning. Keeping my eyes firmly on the stones, I bow to her and sit down.

The chequered board is like a stormy sea with white and black waves chasing and crashing into each other. Towards the four shores they draw back, spin round and head for the skies. As they mingle, they clash and come together in a fierce embrace.

As usual, she says nothing – silence is an impenetrable mystery that all women possess, and hers stifles me. What is she thinking about? Why does she not talk to me? They say women have no memory ... Has she forgotten everything already?

It is true that yesterday evening as we walked down the hill I lacked the courage to take her in my arms. She expected from me the love that a Chinese man has for a Chinese woman. How could I open my heart to her without betraying my country? How could I tell her that we are separated by a mirror, that we are going round in circles in two hostile worlds?

Her stones are soaring now, her moves come faster and

faster, she uses any number of different strategies. What a player!

Suddenly she slows her rhythm.

85

Each move sees my sinking soul take another step downwards. I have always loved the game of go for its labyrinths. Each stone's position evolves as you move the others around it. The relationships between them become more and more complex; they alter and never quite tally with what you had conceived. Go makes a nonsense of your calculations, and defies your imagination. Each new formation is as unpredictable as the alchemy of the clouds and it is a betrayal of what might have been. There is no rest, you're always on the alert, always faster, heading for some part of yourself that is slyer and freer, but also colder, more calculating and more deadly. Go is a game of lies; you surround the enemy with monstrous traps for the sake of the only truth – which is death.

Rather than go home, where Mother is waiting to take me to the doctor, I have resolved to brave its crushing authority.

So, here I am facing the go-table and my stranger.

He looks very ordinary with his slightly outdated tunic, his hat and his glasses, but there is something about him that betrays the change in him. Despite the fact that he has shaved carefully, the powerful growth of his stubble gives his tanned cheeks a bluish shadow. His eyes gleam like two diamonds between his thick black eyelashes and there are thin ellipses of purple under his eyes. I remember Min's eyes showing these same signs after he had climaxed inside me.

Embarrassed, I look away. The other tables on the Square of a Thousand Winds are deserted, the players have left. My countless games of go come rushing back to me: unfamiliar faces merge together in the mask of my opponent's face. He has the nobility of a man who prefers the complexities of the mind to the barbarities of life.

If I leave with Jing I would be entrusting my new life to him. But nothing about him attacts me any more. His dark face used to fire my imagination and his jealousy intoxicated me. The tips of my fingers still recall the smooth, firm feel of his skin that day he gave me a lift on his bicycle. Now he is nothing but a beggar plaguing me.

The convoluted spell that bound Min, Jing and me has evaporated. I was fascinated by a hero with two heads: Jing is nothing without Min, and Min wouldn't have meant anything without Jing. The love of a survivor would stifle me with its weight. How can I explain to him that the only things left between us are a nostalgia for a long-lost happiness and an affectionate form of pity?

But if I don't run away today, my mother will force me to go to the doctor and they will find out why I haven't been well. Huong has chosen to sell herself, but I refuse to see her wearing her expensive clothes and her affable little smile. Min is dead and Jing has been struck down, diminished for ever. This town is a graveyard: why should I stay here? What is keeping me here?

My opponent leans towards me and whispers, 'I'm sorry, I have to go. Can we meet again tomorrow?'

I am devastated by these terribly ordinary words. The game of go has made it possible for me to overcome my pain; one move at a time I have come back to life. If I leave the game now I would be betraying the one man who has remained faithful to me.

86

NIGHT IS falling, reminding me that I have a barracks to get back to and a meeting with Captain Nakamura. The Chinese girl carries on playing in the dark. I am already late, but the thought of being alone with her under a starry sky makes me think breezily, 'I'm sorry, Captain, you'll just have to wait.'

Eventually, with the help of my conscience and my self-discipline, I make up my mind to leave. But she holds me back.

'Please wait.'

She lowers her eyes slowly, her eyelids quivering. She has beauty spots on her face and they seem to flutter to the rhythm of her breathing, like tiny moths.

'Now that we are alone,' she says, 'no one can hear us but the wind. Now, when I close my eyes, I am with you here in the darkness and I can ask you something that I wouldn't dare ask you with my eyes open. Tell me, who are you?'

The Chinese girl's question sets my pulse racing, the blood beating against my temples. It feels as if I have been waiting for this deliverance for an eternity. Does she know my secret? Does she just want to know my name and something about me? I am so choked with different emotions that I cannot speak.

'I have never wondered who my opponents were,' she goes on. 'The men who used to sit where you are now all merged together, and only one game of go stood out from another. Yesterday I saw you for the first time on that hillside. Through your eyes I saw the land in which you were born: an endless white snowfield where trees burn and the flames spread on the wind. The strength of the snow and the fire have turned you into a travelling magician. You heal people by holding their hands between yours, you make them forget the cold, hunger, sickness and war.'

I close my eyes . . . I am inside my Chinese girl's body and I am so far away from her. A poignant shiver of sadness runs through me: I do not deserve this love. I am a spy, an assassin!

She has stopped talking, and the moon rises in the silence between us. I can hear the trees crying and my own icy voice.

'You are wrong, I am just someone passing through who has been captivated by your intelligence. I am like all the other men who have sat down at your go-table and then disappeared. Forgive me if I went too far yesterday afternoon. I can assure you that it was the first time and it will be the last. I respect you. Please forget what you have just said . . . you are too young to judge strangers.'

Her mocking laughter comes as a surprise.

'When we started this game your strategies struck me as strange. I was so intrigued by them that I decided to slip inside your thoughts. With the help of the sheet of paper on which I kept a note of the moves, I cheated. I used to read it over and over again in the rickshaw on the way home. It wasn't to beat you, I wanted to discover you. I visited your soul, I delved in corners you didn't know were there, I became you and I understood that you aren't really yourself.'

I sigh: a few days ago I guessed what she has just admitted to me, and since then winning has not meant anything any more. The game has become a pretext for seeing my opponent, a lie to justify my weakness.

She is right, I do not know how to be myself, I am just a succession of masks.

'Now that you know what I have done,' she says, 'you can stop the game. You can despise me and stop seeing me. You could also challenge me to a new game. It's up to you.'

'Up to me?'

'I will do whatever you want.'

I open my eyes wide with amazement and the girl, this girl who plays go, stares at me intently. The anxious look in her eyes reminds me of how Sunlight looked when she invited me to deflower her.

I am suffocating in the heat and finding it difficult to breathe.

'I will be leaving for the inner territories soon. You can't depend on me any more.'

'I have to leave town too,' she says shakily, 'I want to go to Peking. Please help me!'

I have to make a decision: she is asking me to defy the impossible, and yet all it would take would be a few simple actions. I would just have to raise my arms, take hold of her hands and draw her to me. We could leave and go somewhere else.

I do not know how much time has passed. I am still sitting on my chair, paralysed. The night is so dark that I can hardly see. The darkness chivvies away my shame and encourages me to be irrational, but I do not have the courage to override what fate has in store for us.

I hear myself talking in a hard, hoarse voice and a flat intonation that makes my chest explode with pain.

'I'm sorry. I can't help you.'

A long time later I hear the rustling of her dress: she gets up and moves away.

87

IT IS strange to look round your own room and wonder which are the most precious things in your life. At sixteen I have brushes for calligraphy, paper and phials of ink of very rare quality that were given to me by my grandmother. Every year my parents had four dresses made to measure for me. I also have coats, cloaks, muffs, embroidered shoes, patent-leather shoes, bracelets, earrings, brooches and necklaces. I have school uniforms, sports clothes, boxes of crayons, pens and rubbers. I have toys, hand puppets, shadow puppets and porcelain animals that I used to cry over if I lost them; and books that I loved so much I wanted to take them with me to the grave.

There are valuable pieces of furniture inlaid with mother-of-pearl, a screen covered with embroidered silk, an antique tented bed and a bonsai tree given to me by Cousin Lu. There are mirrors, little boxes of tweezers and manicure kits, a bag of toiletries, antique vases and the calligraphies of my ancestors. There are needles, coloured threads, tins of tea, glasses that still bear the imprint of my lips, sheets impregnated with my smell and pillows that cradled my thoughts. There are the frames around my windows that I used to lean against, and the plants in the garden that I caressed with my straying gaze.

Moon Pearl comes up to tell me that supper is ready. She has grown thinner and her face has lost all its expression. I ask her to stay in my room for a while; she sits down at my dressing table without a word and the tears begin to fall.

My last supper at home is sadly ominous: no one speaks. My parents eat without looking at each other, both nursing the guilt they feel because of Moon Pearl's condition. The cook is so overcome that she drops a pair of chopsticks, and the clatter reawakens my sister's tears. She cries. I can easily imagine the evenings after I have left: a gloomy table where my place will still be laid (a custom that apparently brings back those who are missing); the food that no one touches; my parents' silence; my sister drowning in her own tears.

I stuff a few things into my bag: some pieces of jewellery to sell, two dresses and some cotton wool to absorb the blood that still trickles between my legs.

I put the two pots of stones down on my table. I want to take one white stone and one black stone with me . . . Then I decide that I shouldn't be sentimental about memories.

88

I AM not going back to the Square of a Thousand Winds.

I hardly eat any more, and I drive my body to ever more demanding training, but still it resists exhaustion. There has not been a drop of rain for days and the relentless bronze sun is driving me insane. My love has been transformed into a bestial desire, and in the long, sleepless nights I am like a man slaking his thirst with imaginary water; I sometimes think that I really am touching her skin, I have imagined it so many times. I endlessly draw her face in my mind's eye, her neck, her shoulders, her hands . . . and I invent her breasts, her hips, her buttocks and her open thighs. I imagine the thousand different positions in which I would clasp her to me, each more wild and abandoned than the last. I touch myself, but my member taunts my aching desire, refusing to reach a climax and release me from my pain.

This nocturnal obsession soon seeps into daytime: I have erections while we go for a run, my voice cracks when I give orders, and the hoarse break at the back of my throat conjures the pleasure that the Chinese girl could have given me. To suffer the chafing of her narrow person around my member would have been the most violent form of ecstasy I could ever experience.

One morning, unable to find any form of peace, I go to the Square of a Thousand Winds. It is five o'clock and the trees are whispering in the strong breeze, as if a thousand different draughts and breezes had agreed to meet there at the break of day.

The first player appears, carrying a birdcage in his hand. As he cleans the table and puts down the pots of stones, another man goes over to him and sits down opposite him.

My heart sinks.

That evening, after getting drunk with the Captain, I go and knock on Orchid's door. She has already forgotten all her resentment and slips off her dress within moments. It is a long time since I have touched a woman. In her nudity I see the Chinese girl's nakedness and I discharge into her as violently as emptying the cylinder of a gun.

I wander through the streets in the hope of meeting her, and this tiny town suddenly seems vast. Disappointed, I try a different brothel, but none of the girls parading past does anything for me. Still, I go up to Peony's room with her, and when she smiles she reveals one golden tooth. Her body is fat and very white, and she cries out exuberantly.

At four o'clock in the morning a White Russian girl agrees to let me slap her as I sit astride her. My belt buckle leaves purple streaks across her skin.

Dawn is breaking, a new day just like the other dawns. I shake a rickshaw boy awake and he takes me to the foot of the Hill of the Seven Ruins. Up the hill the tree under which she slept is clothed in rays of purple light, and it stays true to my memory, but the rest of the scene has lost all its poetry. In the middle of the clearing the grass has grown too high and it is beginning to dry out.

Back at the barracks I have forgotten how to harangue my soldiers, how to stand up, even how to sit down. My mind is on other things, somewhere else, nowhere.

That night I am woken by piercing whistles. I open my eyes. My deliverance has come.

The locomotive stands by the platform billowing columns of steam. I push and shove my men, screaming at them to hurry up, then I get in and pull the door closed behind me. I suddenly realise that I have forgotten to say goodbye to Captain Nakamura.

89

PEKING, CITY of dust.

Jing comes back with the newspapers under his arms, but every day his face is a little darker: the negotiations with the Japanese army have failed and war is very close. Chiang Kai-shek's central government is calling upon the Chinese nation to resist the foreign invasion. The exodus has already started in the streets, thousands of the people of Peking streaming towards the south with their belongings bagged up on their backs.

Ever since we arrived here, Jing has forbidden me to leave the hotel room. When he is here, I refuse to get up. He keeps blaming himself for dragging me nearer to danger and death, and his guilt makes him irritable. He is becoming disgusting, he is uglier by the day and his hair is too long; he bites his fingernails and eats like an animal.

I lie wrapped in a sheet as white as a shroud and argue with him over anything: the noodles are too warm, the tea is too bitter, the mosquitoes. The terrible heat drives me on to crush him with my constant complaining. Most of the time he responds with contemptuous silence, but sometimes he gets annoyed and in his rage his face goes bright red, his whole body shakes and he throws himself at me and tries to strangle me.

'Go on, kill me!' I scream. 'Just like you killed your friends!'

His face distorts into a snarl and I see Min's ghost flit through his eyes.

I end up giving him my cousin's address, and ask him to bring Lu to me. Jing is angry at first, but when I tell him that Lu is married he goes off to find him quite happily.

When he has left I can breathe at last. Without Jing the room feels airy and full of light. I get up, wash my face and then go and comb my hair over by the open window.

Our hotel in Peking is a large single-storey building with the rooms arranged around a square courtyard with a jujube tree growing in the middle of it. On the other side of the wall, out on the street, there are children chattering to each other in pure Peking dialect. In their intonations I pick out the same accent as the man who played go. His was slightly different: instead of rolling his r's, he pronounced them with his lips. My thoughts go back to the Hill of the Seven Ruins where he watched over me as I slept. On the Square of a Thousand Winds he would sometimes open out his fan, but it wasn't to cool himself, he managed to beat it so that the gentle breeze wafted onto my face. I feel my heart constrict at the memory. I still don't understand why he said no. Why do people want to run away when they recognise their own happiness?

There are planes flying overhead, then I hear wave

after wave of thundering explosions. People are screaming in the streets, saying the Japanese are threatening to
flatten the whole city.

The air is drier in Peking than in our Manchurian
towns. Everything gleams, shimmers and sparkles in the
white sunlight and then is swallowed up into an ashen
grey. I have only just got up, but I am already tired again.
Peking, the city of my ancestors, is a dream from which I
cannot wake up.

I go back to bed and drop in and out of sleep. I see my
parents' faces and feel overwhelmed by the sight of them.
Then I make my way slowly to the Square of a Thousand
Winds, towards the go-table. I feel so happy when I pick
up the ice-cool stones in my hands. The Stranger is there,
steady as a statue. Our game continues, evolving along its
convoluted route towards the Land of Purity.

At night Jing listens to the tumult of successive
skirmishes and falls asleep leaning against the wall. I am
suddenly woken by him screaming in horror. He has his
hands to his head and is struggling like a man possessed. I
get out of bed and hold him in my arms. How can I leave
him?

At dawn he shakes me awake. He has made up his
mind: it is better to risk dying under the bombs and
heading south than waiting for the massacre here. I regret
ever having paid any attention to my impulses: I wanted
to embrace freedom and now I am Jing's prisoner.

'I must talk to my cousin, he's my only relation here.
Keep looking for him. Let's find him and go with him.'

Jing's expression darkens.

'I lied earlier when I said he had moved house. I saw
his wife and she's gone almost mad. Lu's abandoned her
and signed up for the army. He may already be dead.'

'You're lying! Give me my cousin's address back.'

'Here, have it, you'll see for yourself.'

I know that Jing is telling the truth and I cry out in despair.

'I want to go back to Manchuria. We've got to go our separate ways. I'm going home, I'm going back to my game of go.'

'It's too late. There's no more public transport. All the trains have been requisitioned by the Japanese army. You don't have the choice now, you'll have to come with me.'

'You're jealous of Min,' I spit at him. 'You've taken me away from my town to erase him from my memory.'

'Min slept with you for fun. Don't forget that Tang was everything to him, his big sister, his teacher and his wife!'

Jing thinks this will hurt me, but I burst out laughing.

'You're wrong. Min's over! I've dug a grave in my heart and buried him. I never loved him, anyway. We made a beautiful couple and I was flattered by that. I liked seeing you both jealous. I now realise that it was just vanity – do you understand – the vanity of becoming a woman.'

Jing's face darkens and he stares at me coldly.

'You toyed with my affection and I can forgive you that,' he says. 'Your body is tainted now and no one will marry a girl who's no longer a virgin. I'm the only person in this whole huge world who loves you, and I'll take the woman who was defiled by my best friend! I'm all you've got and you're mine!'

Min said that my body belonged to him, he insisted on having exclusive rights to my body even as he gave himself to other women. Jing is like him ... The accumulation of emotion brings tears to my eyes.

'There is someone else who loves me,' I say, 'and I've only just realised that I loved him without knowing it. I am going back to the town of A Thousand Winds for him. He's waiting for me.'

'Liar! Who is he? Where's he from? Can I have his name, please? Come on, tell me.'

I suddenly realise that I don't even know his name. I don't know anything about him except his soul. Seeing my hesitation, Jing calms down a little and takes me in his arms. I slap him, but he manages to kiss my forehead.

'Come with me,' he says, 'don't be a child. We'll start a new life in Nanking.'

90

CLOUDS OF flies hover in the air.
On the plain the shells have carved deep craters, the fields have been ravaged and there are bodies everywhere. Some still have waxy faces, lying with their mouths open. Others are just piles of flesh mangled into the soil.

Our unit slowly crosses this vast cemetery, and I realise that some of our soldiers fell into an enemy trap and fought to the last man. The sun is making me feel nauseous, and at that moment I understand that our fight against the terrorists in Manchuria was just a game of hide-and-seek. Only now do I grasp for the first time the enormity and horror of war.

We are caught in a storm of explosions in the middle of a deserted village. I throw myself to the ground as the bullets rain down onto earth whitened by weeks of drought. After a brief exchange of fire, we conclude that the unit attacking us consists of just a few diehard individuals who have stayed behind to hamper our progress. The bugle sounds the attack, and the Chinese scatter like rabbits used as targets in a shooting competition. I aim at the fastest man, who is just about to reach the edge of the woods, and pull the trigger. He crumples at the foot of a tree.

At midday there is a second violent attack; the Chinese are so drunk with despair that they have become ferocious. I lie full-length on a sloping piece of ground with the burning sun on my back, and I catch a waft of a sweet smell, which reminds me of the girl who played go. In front of me a soldier who has been hit in the back rolls on the ground screaming. I recognise him as one of my men, the one I am most fond of – we have just celebrated his nineteenth birthday.

I wanted to bury the boy after the battle, but the order to march on is given and I have to leave his body to the attentions of the next regiment. Inequality goes with us beyond the grave. The luckiest are burned on the battlefield, and others thrown into a ditch, but the most unfortunate are gathered up by the Chinese, who cut off their heads and parade them around on stakes.

This first day of warfare feels like a long dream. Nothing touches me, neither the atrocities of the fighting, nor the exhausting march, nor the deaths of my soldiers. I wander through a padded world where life and death are equally meaningless. For the first time the military adventure has failed to inspire me: we go to our fates just as salmon struggle back upstream – there is no beauty or grandeur in it.

That evening the medical officer notices that I am sullen and withdrawn and he diagnoses sunstroke. I let my men wrap my head in a cool, damp towel and lie down on a bale of straw, staring at the dark ceiling of the requisitioned cottage. I am disgusted with myself.

We are woken by whistling and explosions in the early hours of the morning. We respond with grenades, and then both sides resort to machine guns. In all the cacophony we suddenly recognise the bugle sounding the attack.

The division that has just attacked us is Japanese, a misunderstanding which cost us the lives of several men.

91

A CAMP fire crackling, Jing snoring, and all around me there are hundreds of other refugees sleeping. Humans in exodus are like herds of deer fleeing a drought, they are thin and sick, and their sleep is as heavy as the worries they carry on their shoulders.

I take a pair of scissors from my bag and cut my hair as short as the strength in my arms permits. I tie my two plaits together with a ribbon and lay them next to Jing, then I climb over ten sleeping bodies and disappear into the night.

In a wood I take off my dress and slip on the clothes I have stolen from Jing. Behind the trees the dawn casts its pale light over the Peking plain. I walk in the opposite direction to the refugees who have been moving since daybreak. The women, weighed down with bundles of belongings, drag their children in one hand and their goats in the other. From time to time the unmistakable screams of new-born babies ring out. There are men carrying an ageing parent on their backs; others are luckier and have been able to put them in a rickshaw. An old woman of nearly a hundred clutches a chicken in her arms as she teeters forwards on her bound feet.

My heart has been broken by a succession of scenes like this ever since we fled Peking. I don't regret following Jing into this upheaval; thanks to him, I have seen the inner strength of a people driven from its own land. The tenacity of this march south is like a silent protest against death. These men and women form a wave of hatred mingled with hope. This furious force will stay with me to the very ends of my lonely progress.

I am like them − I want life. I want to go back to Manchuria, to find my house and my go-table. I will return to the Square of a Thousand Winds and wait for the Unknown Player, the Stranger. I know he will come to me . . . one afternoon . . . as he did that first time.

At midday I sit under a tree by the side of the road and I eat a three-day-old piece of bread one crumb at a time. The droning of the aeroplanes and the distant explosions contrast starkly with the silence of the steadily advancing crowd of people.

Within that human river the first Chinese soldiers appear. In their blood-splattered uniforms and their faces darkened with smoke, they remind me of the soldiers who invaded our house in 1931 after fleeing the Japanese: their eyes betray their exhaustion and the peculiar coldness of those who have left their fellows to the slaughter.

'Peking has fallen! Hurry up, we must flee.'

'The Japanese are coming! The demons are coming!'

People begin screaming and crying. I catch sight of Jing running with his halting limp in the opposite direction to the refugees, and I hide behind a tree. He passes a stone's throw from me and I hear him asking a woman whether she has seen a pale young girl with her hair cut short and dressed as a boy. His voice cracks and, holding my plaits in his hand, he spits on the ground and curses me as he calls my name.

His words cut me to the quick: 'How could you make me suffer like this, I have been to hell and back already!'

Eventually he moves away.

An aeroplane that has been circling overhead for a while suddenly drops a bomb, and then another. The explosions throw me to the ground and I lose consciousness. When I come to, there are people running in every direction like a line of ants disturbed by someone crossing their path.

I get up and notice that my arm is bleeding. The roaring of the engines in the sky becomes louder and louder: there are more planes coming towards us! I run over into a field.

The Japanese bomb the road. I wander through the fields not knowing where to hide, my head is spinning and my injured arm dangles heavily by my side. When am I going to wake up from this nightmare?

Before nightfall I make out a village on the horizon and I hurry towards it. When I get there it is eerily silent. In the darkness I can just see the doors hanging open and broken pieces of furniture strewn across the streets. A little further on I come across some bodies: four peasants skewered with bayonets. Inside the houses there is not one living creature, not one grain of rice, not one piece of straw to fuel an oven. After the massacre the Japanese army must have taken everything.

I don't have the strength to carry on any further, so I go into one of the cottages. Remembering a remedy my mother used to talk about, I cover my wound with cold ashes before binding it with some cloth torn from my shirt. I huddle against the cold, dark stove and burst into tears.

In the morning I am woken by a terrible racket, then I hear men shouting at each other in some incomprehensible language.

I open my eyes.

There are soldiers pointing their guns at me.

92

Pᴇᴋɪɴɢ ɪs conquered.

We have been sent orders to scour the countryside for spies and injured Chinese soldiers. They must all be executed.

This morning my men came across a questionable individual; he is dwarfed by the student's clothes he is wearing and insists obstinately on staring at the ground and remaining insolently silent.

The soldiers are charging their rifles. Lieutenant Hayashi, who is running the operation with me, raises his arm, draws his sabre and says, 'You have always boasted about your family sabre, which dates back to the sixteenth century. Mine was forged a hundred years later, but it was known at the time as the "Head-slicer". I'll give you a demonstration.'

The soldiers are charged with excitement at the thought of this display, and they click their tongues and call to each other in their anticipation.

Hayashi adopts the samurai stance that he has learned from ancient engravings, spreading his feet, flexing his knees and bringing the sabre up over his head.

The prisoner looks up slowly.

I suddenly feel unsteady on my feet.

'Wait!' I cry, and I run over to the young man to wipe his face, which has been blackened by mud and smoke. I can make out the tear-shaped beauty spots.

'Don't touch me,' she screams.

'A woman,' Hayashi cries, putting his sabre back in its sheath and pushing past me to knock the prisoner over and put his hand inside her trousers.

My heart turns to ice. It's her! What's she doing here in this village? When did she leave Manchuria?

'A woman!' Hayashi confirms excitedly.

The young girl struggles, screaming shrilly. He slaps her twice, takes off her shoes and pulls down her trousers. He undoes his own belt and the soldiers, mesmerised, form a circle around him.

'Out of the way!' he orders them. 'You'll each have a turn!'

'You idiot!' I say, throwing myself at the Lieutenant. He turns to me furiously, but when he sees my pistol aimed at his forehead he starts to laugh good-naturedly.

'Okay,' he says, 'you'd better have her first. After all, you found her.'

I say nothing. Thinking he understands why, he whispers, 'It's the first time, isn't it? If you don't want to do it in public, look, go over to the temple. I'll keep watch by the door.'

Hayashi takes me over to the nearby temple, while two soldiers carry the girl and throw her to the ground. They shut the door, giggling to each other.

She is shaking from head to toe. I take off my tunic to cover her bare legs.

'Don't be frightened,' I say in Chinese.

My voice seems to disturb her, she opens her eyes wide and scrutinises me. A terrible agony floods across her features and suddenly she spits in my face before falling back to the ground in tears.

'Kill me! Kill me!'

Hayashi knocks on the door and I can hear him sniggering.

'Hurry up, Lieutenant. My soldiers can't wait much longer!'

I hold my Chinese girl in my arms. She bites my shoulder and, despite the pain, I hold my cheek next to hers. Tears spill from my eyes and I whisper, 'Forgive me, forgive me . . .'

Her only reply is to scream hysterically, 'Kill me, please, I beg you. Kill me, don't let me live!'

'Lieutenant,' Hayashi calls from the other side of the door, 'you're taking your time. Hurry up. Don't be so selfish!'

I grab my pistol and I hold it to the Chinese girl's temple. She looks up at me and there is no longer any fear in her eyes. Now she has the indifference she always used to accord to strangers.

I shudder and press my weapon a little more firmly.

'Do you recognise me?'

She closes her eyes.

'I know that you hate me, I know you won't forgive me. At this moment, I couldn't care less that you despise me. I'm going to kill you and I will kill myself afterwards. For your sake I'm going to turn my back on this war and betray my own country. For your sake I will be unworthy of my own parents, I will sully my ancestors' honour. My name will never be inscribed in the Temple of Heroes. It will be cursed instead.'

I cover her in kisses and now there are tears on her cheeks. She lets me kiss her without resisting.

The ground trembles as the men drum it with their rifle butts.

'Have you finished, Lieutenant? I'm going to count to three and then I'm coming in! One . . .'

I now don't have time to ask her why she left her country, why she cut her beautiful hair. I have a thousand questions to ask her and I won't utter a single one of them. I have never known how to speak to her of my love.

'Two . . .'

'Don't worry,' I whisper in her ear, 'I'll follow you. I'll look after you in the afterlife.'

She opens her eyes and stares at me:

'My name is Song of the Night.'

But I have already pulled the trigger. Her dark eyes quiver, her pupils dilate, the blood spurts from her temples. With her eyes wide open, she falls backwards to the ground.

The door opens and I can hear footsteps behind me. I realise with despair that I don't even have time to cut open my entrails as would befit a samurai.

I put the blood-splattered pistol into my mouth.

A loud noise, the ground trembling beneath my feet.

I fall onto the girl who played go. Her face looks pinker than it did earlier. She is smiling. I know that we will go on with our game up there.

I try very hard to keep my eyes open so that I can look at my beloved.